Four Months Past Florence

Emily Paige Wilson

Andrews McMeel
PUBLISHING®

Andrews McMeel Publishing
a division of Andrews McMeel Universal
1130 Walnut Street, Kansas City, Missouri 64106

www.andrewsmcmeel.com

23 24 25 26 27 SHO 10 9 8 7 6 5 4 3 2 1

ISBN: 978-1-5248-8133-7

Library of Congress Control Number: 2022945727

Editor: Danys Mares
Art Director: Julie Barnes
Production Editor: Brianna Westervelt
Production Manager: Chuck Harper

Illustrations by Sam Ward

—for Roy and Joseph,

who sheltered us during the storm

I. Two Weeks Before Florence

Monday, August 27th, 2018

I Consult My Vision Board before the First Day of School

Portraits of my favorite journalists—
    Diane Sawyer, Melissa Harris-Perry.
    Rachel Maddow and Lisa Ling.

    Women who've covered wars and turmoil
    with their words, who've made the world listen.

A mock medallion thumb-tacked up by its wide blue ribbon—
    The Peabody Award—
        George Foster's stern face etched in gold.

        The highest aspiration I hold,
        to win the real deal one day,
        to do enough good with my words
        that I'm heard on a global scale.

College seals from schools
with competitive journalism programs—

    Chapel Hill and Columbia. NYU.
    Application dates and graduation rates.

Photos with Lola Sun all the way back to third grade.
    Printed screenshots of our longest Snapchat streak.

And the masthead of our school newspaper, *The Bloom*,
my byline highlighted—

    Millie Willard.

    Junior.

    Weatherwoman.

Lola Sun Honks Her Horn from the Driveway

Lola Sun—my best friend and astrology aficionado.
Aquarius sun; Aries moon.

> Creative and patient, except
> for the twilight flare-ups of her temper when tested,
> her sudden impulses to sulk.

> She blames the stars for all our shortcomings.
> Wears red heart-shaped plastic frames
> and splatters faux freckles across her nose.

She lugs us off to school in her lime-green Volkswagen bug,
> my ride or die until I'm ready
> to trade in my permit for a license of my own.

As she drives, she passes me today's star chart,
> the curve and shine of constellations
> stenciled in the corner.

What the Stars Say

The moon makes her slow way through Taurus,
the silver thrill of romance
           and all its messy ramifications.

Speak sweetly today.
Floss flowers through your hair.

Couple compliments with small gestures—
nothing grand—
      until Mercury finally pushes past
      its post-retrograde shadow,

      the cold no-man's land
      of miscommunication and mayhem.

Ugh, It's Always Mercury,

I say.

Lola Sun secures
a junior parking spot,
slots her car squarely
beneath the sway
of a Sabal palm.

Girl, she says.

Her heart-shaped frames
slide down her nose,

big brown eyes
bubble above them.

You have no idea.

Homeroom at Magnolia High

All of us newspaper nerds
hang out for homeroom.

Our office, an old teachers' lounge.

A row of outdated computers.
A thrift store couch threadbare and stained.

Broken-down Keurig that brews
lukewarm coffee in sporadic spurts.

In a small school of seven hundred students
in the nowhere cool coastal town of Magnolia, South Carolina,

we may just be another club to everyone else,
but we take pride in our work.

We're a professional publication
and expect to be treated as such.

Perhaps Our Logo Best Represents

our journalistic approach.

Lola Sun created the art herself—
    precise pen work and weepy watercolors.

Airbrushed magnolia petals of cream curl upwards,
capped in magnificent strokes of lavender and gold.

    A beetle wraps itself around them,
    blue-black shellacked shell.
    Mandibles poised
        to pinch.

Magnolias are such an old species,
    they evolved before bees,
    before butterflies and other,
    more beautiful winged things.

So it's up to the lowly beetle
to spread the flower's pollen.

        And that's our approach to journalism.

          Make it bold—open as a magnolia bursting—
          but don't shy away from the grunt work.

            Don't be afraid
            to get down and dirty
            in the slick and shit of it all.

Our Masthead

is pretty much a list of me and my closest friends.

Sports Editor: Todd Turlington

Todd is a powerhouse of sports reports.
They shoot statistics off the top of their head
faster than fly balls.

A fair-weather fan, Todd has a new favorite
football team for every day of the week
and dyes their hair accordingly.

It's the Seahawks for now—and a matching mess
　　of electric green and navy tresses that fade to teal.

Todd is nonbinary and serves as secretary of the GSA.
　　They work hard to make the world of sports—
　　and our school—safer and more inclusive.

Layout Editor, Web Design: Stephen Hassan

Stephen made his first Squarespace page at the age of five
to feature all his Lego designs.

Analytical and a guru with graphics, rumor has it
Google's already offered him a post-graduation internship.

We publish in print once a semester,
but Stephen updates our website daily.

He's our deadline, our color-coded to-do list,
the guiding light who gets us to the presses on time.

Photographer: Maya Nickleson

Maya's sharp eye frames every moment as a scene.
With a click, she creates
        wordless stories
                full of grit and grace and glory.

Her current portfolio is full of mixed media portraits
of her three-year-old niece
                collaged into the costumes
        of historic high priestesses and queens.

Maya's signature style is to sprinkle gold glitter
into her fro—she shines down the hall,
        a string of sparkles between all her classes.
        She's both the paparazzi and the star.

Arts Editor, Horoscopes: Lola Sun Li Jing

I love Lola Sun.

Not the most professional way to start her profile,
but still.

Lola Sun's parents have all her childhood doodles framed—
red scribbles displayed in the hallway of their home,
sloppy crayon spirals on construction paper.

        Finger-painted faces and the first Chinese characters
        she ever calligraphed in onyx ink.

        With each weekly horoscope and comic strip,
        she keeps us entertained with stars and art.

Weatherwoman: Millie Willard

And then there's me.

A mess of auburn tresses,
complexion so pale and pink
Lola Sun says my Fenty foundation shade
would be named *Not Quite Rose Quartz*
were I even to wear makeup at all.

Mama said she knew I'd be an investigative reporter
when I was four and she caught me
    snooping in her closet for Christmas presents.

    I rambled on and raised Cain—

        Did you buy these presents?
        Are the elves just pretend?

        Mama was too amused by my meddling
        to go through the pain of punishment.

            And I'm even more tenacious now,
            covetous for cover stories,
            bored by storm fronts and clouds.

The Downside to My Weatherwoman Role

is I'm made for so much more.

I'm meant to break stories,
not write boring reports
on this season's tropical storms:

Alberto,

Beryl,

Chris,

Debby,

Ernesto.

No more than a string
of misbehaving children,
bored and churning
up trouble.

Emily Paige Wilson

Finally, Our Editor-in-Chief

Maria Renée Robles.

Now, I'm not saying she's perfect, but
    she's definitely gorgeous.

    Skin the color of sherry topaz,
    a light brown stone that gleams peach when sunlight-struck.

Her mother's Mexican, father's Puerto-Rican,
and when she speaks Spanish, there's a music
in her voice, a movement and meter
      as if sounds were water.

      As if you could dance
      in the puddles of her dropped words.

And she's smart.

    When she ran for Miss Magnolia last year,
    she stunned everyone
    with her less-than-standard pageant answer
    to the question:

      What's the most important trait for a young woman
        to have today?

    Camera panned in—
    her lip gloss all diamond and dare—
    she said,

      Women are not a monolith.

      There is not one singular trait we need
      to succeed or survive.

Some of us fight racism,
transphobia, ableism.

Some want careers or families
or both.

Some have vaginas, some don't—

It was then she was dragged off stage,
    the audience a mix of audacious applause and grandmotherly gasps.

Needless to say, she lost the pageant—
    too progressive a speech for Charleston County—

    but she went viral.

With her fifteen minutes
and few thousand retweets of fame,

    Maria Renée auctioned off her pale blue pageant gown
    and donated all proceeds to the ACLU.

See, She's Pretty Much Perfect

And I need her to trust
that I'm fit to follow in her editorial footsteps,

that I'm worthy of her red pen,

once she graduates this spring.

We Pitch Feature Stories All Morning

Todd, of course, wants sports—
a double-pager on the proposed
stadium upgrades.

Maya, who's mad this money won't fund
a new art studio darkroom, disagrees.

    I'm about to open my mouth,
    throw out an idea—

when Maria Renée sighs dramatically,
a symptom of what Lola Sun calls
her Sagittarius moon.

    C'mon, you guys, she begs the room.
    Be more creative!

    You've had all summer to track leads.
    I want real story suggestions,
    not something your grandmother
    would scroll through on her newsfeed.

    How am I supposed to have
    confidence in this team
    when I leave?

When She Leaves

When Maria Renée leaves in the spring,
I'll only have one chance
to secure the editor spot.

    See, this isn't a position
    we vote on every semester.

        No rotational slot,
        no taking turns
        until everyone learns the ropes.

It's cutthroat—
a lifer seat appointed
by the last editor's authority.

        This cuts down on confusion,
        ensures continuity.

        Some students never even see
        an editor opening—

            it's a rare occurrence,
            like twin tornados
            twisting through town.

When Maria Renée leaves,
it'll be my last chance
to fulfill my dream.

What the Kitchen Smells Like When I Come Home

from school and Mama's been cooking.

> Oven-roasted okra.
> Rosemary and sage sautéed in mushroom gravy.

> Mashed yams and eggless pecan pies.

Mama cooks at The Anchor,
the hippest and most expensive hotel in town.
> Worked her way up from waitressing
> to become head chef Heather Grace.

Tenacious and talented, she tests
the boundaries of vegan Southern cuisine—

> jackfruit stewed in barbeque sauce,
> mac 'n' cheese made with cashews and yeast.

Even though she's a small-town success story,
she still wears the same shade of red polish
from her waitress days—

> *Check Together or Separate?*

> A high shine reminder of her mission—

> > to make home-cooking plant-based,
> > each plate hearty, yet healthy.

> > To balance
> > hope and humility.

We End Our Evenings Watching the Local News

Channel Five and my favorite newscaster—

Felicia Fitz.

Quaffed blonde hair.
A wide, white smile.
Streaks of blush hit high on her cheekbones.

Her golden hoop earrings glisten
as she leans in for interviews,

always listening for her next scoop.

Felicia Fitz is a paved interstate in a town of red dirt roads.
She's a quick-footed fox in a field of rundown hunting dogs.

She didn't come to play,
and the whole town listens
to what she has to say.

Mama Hates Felicia, Though

Thinks she meddles too much—
    makes Blue Ridge Mountains outta mole hills—

    but Mama doesn't realize every story needs its spin
    if it's gonna rise above all the white noise.

I haven't pinned her portrait to my vision board
on account of Mama bad-mouthin' her,
but that's where she belongs.

Just Between Us,

the real reason Mama stays so sore on the subject
is she thinks Felicia tried to sabotage her cooking career.

A few years ago, Channel Five
ran a series of live restaurant reviews.

Filming behind-the-scenes footage
of Mama's pristine kitchen,

the camera crew panned in on
one lone palmetto bug scurrying
its hurried way across the floor.

Felicia was quick to quip,
Seems we serve a little
animal protein after all?

The comment didn't slow sales,
        didn't make The Anchor fail
        its next sanitation review,

                but Mama has nursed that hurt
                same as if it were a bruise.

And I ain't never heard the end of it.

Homeroom

Two strange occurrences happen this morning,
like the stirring when warm and cold fronts meet.

First, Maria Renée's seat is empty.

At 7:37.

At 7:43.

Even at 7:45
as the bell rings.

Secondly, Lola Sun and Todd
pass notes

—like old school—

folded paper and the soft scratch of pen.

I surreptitiously slide behind them,
pretend I'm on a path to the Keurig

to see if I can sneak a peek
as Todd unfolds the newest note.

Lola Sun has drawn two koi fish circling,
one's tail almost touching the other's head.

The moon is waxing,
letting us have less
than a quarter of its light.

This affects Pisces in particular,
but don't set the spare bedroom up

21

for the guests of gloom and doom
before they even knock.

Don't let your fantasy fish
outswim your reality fish.

Allow them to circle.
Allow them symmetry.

The fish scales look like small hearts.

Since I Have Nothing Better to Do,

I draft weather reports for our website.

> *There is nothing to report. Literally nothing. This is sooooooooo*
> *boring. Boring rhymes with snoring rhymes with a calm and sunny*
> *morning. If I were Felicia Fitz, how would I spin sunshine into a*
> *storm worth reporting?*

Clearly not my best work,
    but I rewrite these lines,

    buy time until either thunder
    or the first bell strikes—

        or maybe an earthquake to shake things up,
            a small one—more tremors than terror—

        when my phone pings.

        An unexpected message from Maria Renée
        blinks through the screen's blue light.

Maria Renée's Text

Hey, Millie!

Super last second, I know,
but could you please do The Morning Minute for me?

I took first period off
for a college Skype interview.

> *Early decision's sneaking up!*

The notes are in the file folder—
ask Stephen if you can't find them.

Thank you and good luck!

I Grab the Notes,

charge out the door,
and march to Principal Keys's office
in triumphant yet measured steps—

    mumble practice runs
    underneath my breath,
    different versions of my voice.

Which one will sound right
when spoken into the mic:

    a more demur purr of words

    or a bright, bombastic projection,
    fireworks crackling into the static?

The Morning Minute is usually
an editor-exclusive gig,
so I try not to wig out.

Notes in hard-knuckled hand,
I inhale the hallway scent
of chalk and sweaty sneakers.

    I knock on the front office door,

        a slight tremble in the tenor—

ready for my debut.

Principal Keys Is a Popular Guy

And for good reason.

You could trace the roots
of his family tree in this town for days
and still not find half the interesting facts,
lose all your time in its unwinding branches.

>   Like how his great-grandfather
>   was Magnolia's first official black Baptist pastor.

>   Or how his sister's hair salon is so famous
>   she was once visited by the Obamas.

Keys also made a name for himself as principal
because his policies have improved the school.

>   He bought us better textbooks,
>   traded in-school suspension
>   for counselors and meditation,

>   and—boom—the graduation rate grew by 23 percent.

I smile at him now as he opens the door.

>   Try to wait patiently
>   as he finishes his own announcements first

>   —praise for the teacher of the week,
>   dress code policy updates—

>   until he finally slides the mic my way.

>   *And here with The Morning Minute*
>   *is our very own Millie Willard.*

The Echo of My Voice

over the intercom
    makes me electric.

I banish the high-pitched swerve of nerves
and run through the notes.

Everything goes so well at first
as I read off the prepared words

    —student council minutes,
        sports scores from summer games—

        until I see something suspicious.

           Something that makes me
           go off script.

To an Untrained Eye,

it's just a few fast-food wrappers,
wrinkled and tossed in the trash,
yesterday's date in faded black marker.

But to a reporter, it's a story.

I announce:

And some of y'all might be surprised to hear
that while the rest of us participated
in the cafeteria's mandatory Meatless Mondays

—bacon-less breakfasts,
bean burritos for lunch—

I, Millie Willard, can provide eyewitness testimony
that the front office smuggled contraband sausage biscuits
into school yesterday.

This is deception at the highest level,
treachery—

Keys seizes the mic from me immediately,
says, *Thank you, Millie.*
That will be all.

His eyes sparkle harshly,
    but
        a slight grin
        twitches his lip.

He sends me out with the threat of detention,
but I'm undeterred.

Blowback is a risk every reporter runs.

Texts Come in Immediately

Lola Sun: *Giiiiiiiiirl, I'm dying!*
    Take that, Mercury!

Todd: *Millie!!!!!! WTF?!?!?!?!*

Maya: *hahahaha that was awesome*
way to highlight the hypocrisy
way to stick it to the man

Stephen: *If you get expelled,*
    you'll still have to meet deadline.

And then Lola Sun again:

        You know Maria Renée's gonna flip, right?

The Rest of the School Day

is as suspended and charged
as a dark sky that threatens thunder.

I wait all afternoon for the boom—

Maria Renée to hear what's happened
and either punish me with proofreading assignments
or praise my bold and brazen reporting;

Mama to threaten me with an ass-whoopin'
on account of me misbehaving—

but the day stays post-storm silent,
the eerie kind that settles thick as fog.

Except online, where lightning strikes left and right.

I can't help but be pleased
as I see students lip-synching to me
all across TikTok,

exaggerated facial features
as they reenact *deception at the highest level*—
fingers wagging at the screen.

Treachery!

Treachery!

I could get used to this—
this attention and affirmation,
this feeling of being seen.

In the Evening,

the thunder finally thrashes.

> After a dinner of braised chickpeas and sweet potato mash,
> Mama's voice calls me from my pre-cal problems.

> *Millie*, she says,

> *The sheriff's here,*

> *and he wants to see you.*

It's the Sheriff's Deputy to Be Exact

Garrett Greenfield—
    rising star in local law enforcement.

    Brown eyes, lashes thick and black.
    Olive-tinted skin
    that always appears wind-chapped.

    Dark hair chopped short
    like the crops of a cautious farmer
    afraid of too little rain,

    but with his wide smile,
    his cheeks flush plump as pumpkins,
    the first treat of harvest season.

    Twenty-eight-year-old young gun
    who won hearts as a hometown hero.

        He helped old Mrs. Marguerite clean up
        after a kitchen fire caught real bad—

        one of her prize-winning blueberry pies
        'bout burned her whole house down.

Garrett's got a politician's charm
without any of the crookedness.

Rumor has it he's gunning to run for sheriff
once old Mr. Beatty retires.

        And here he is now
        at our front door.

I Should Probably Also Mention

Garrett's my second cousin,
and his evening visits to our house
aren't that infrequent.

Mama thinks it's a hoot to introduce him that way—

Millie, sheriff's here to see you!
—and although it gets old,
adults hate being told they ain't funny,

so I fake laugh at Mama's tired jokes.

She cracks her own self up,
bright red hair she handed down to me
jostling with her jilted inhales,
hands on her belly as it expands with laughter.

Garrett rolls his eyes with me—
he's young enough to be on my side of humor.

But that still doesn't address the weather system
taking shape in the room.

What exactly does he know about The Morning Minute?

Is there trouble brewing,
and am I about to get it?

Garrett and My Daddy Used to Be Real Close,

before Daddy passed away in a car crash.

I was only three, but Garrett was fifteen
and Daddy had been teaching him to drive.

> That's why it came as such a surprise when,
> alone one night, Daddy got blindsided
> by a hazardous hairpin turn.

> > His '89 Ford F-150 spun out and knotted 'round
> > an old oak tree on Highway 53.

> Daddy must have been preoccupied,
> something heavy on his mind—
> > because he'd driven that turn many times before.

Once Daddy passed, Mama's friends from college
stayed with us a while: Ellis and Thayer.

> They slept in the spare bedroom,
> Garrett on the couch.

> > Ain't no one wanted to leave Mama alone
> > with her grief and a toddler all tumbles and tantrums.

Had there been a *CAUTION* sign at the accident's scene,
Garrett thinks things would've turned out different.

City council didn't act.
The sheriff's office didn't act.

And the South Carolina Department of Transportation?
They didn't act.

Not 'til they had to trace the dark tracks
of Casey's tread marks—the mistake
of his slammed brakes—

did they finally take citizen concerns seriously.
Too much red tape for one damn yellow sign.

Unspoken between us—
the belief

that had Garrett been sheriff,
had I been a journalist
reporting on this story—

how the city needed this sign—

maybe we could have acted in time.
Maybe we could've saved Daddy's life.

Now Garrett Looks after Me,

Holds me accountable,
scolds me for bad behavior
    like a substitute father figure.

He tells me stories about before I was born—

    how Heather Grace and Casey Willard
    were voted cutest couple at the county fair two years runnin',
    when Mama was young and strung honeysuckle in her wild hair.

        Casey was so excited waiting for you, Garrett's told me.
        Heather Grace wanted to call you Amelia,
        but Casey settled on Millie—
                it still meant ambition;
                it still sounded cute;

        but he wanted to give you
        a name with strong Southern roots.

It Was after Daddy Died

that Mama started to measure time
    in four-month blocks.

A waitress still, she said she saw
four garlic bulbs strung together
above the restaurant's cellar door,

    four copper pots waiting to be washed,

        four stowaway ladybugs
        leafing through chopped cilantro.

She started with four seconds—then days—
    then challenged her grief
    to a four-month streak.

She told herself, *Four months from now,*
    I won't wake up crying every day.

        Four months from now,
        this grief won't reek like compost rot.

        Four months from now,
        I'll trade in these tips and nightly shifts
        for a chef's hat, crisp and clean.

It doesn't always work right away.

    Sometimes she has to add a second
    four-month block—
        sometimes even a third—

    but it's always four months forward.

I Should Probably Also Mention One More Thing

While Garrett's a hometown hero
to most of Magnolia,

   local law enforcement
   hasn't protected everyone equally,
   especially here in the South.

   How could they
   when their history stems
   first from slave patrols and then Jim Crow?

And I only know this
because of Principal Keys—

   he refused to let our school's pedagogy
   be plagued by revisionist history.

   Without him, we'd probably still be taught
   the Civil War was about states' rights.

      Without Keys, there'd be a lot more
      prejudice and privilege left unchecked.

It's Not until Garrett Says Goodbye

and leaves for the night
that I breathe a sigh of relief.

If I was gonna get in trouble for The Morning Minute,
    the moment has clearly passed.

Every Hurricane Season

is a parade of precaution—
a storm surge of weather reports.

Which ones will evade us,
which ones will make us evacuate.

This is the price of coastal living—
the semi-precious metal sunsets ablaze every day,
the fresh seafood and beachside porches.

Every time the weather warms, these incessant warnings.

The National Weather Service's website
has all of them laid out—
mapped models of tropical storms.

From here, they're just spirals off the coast,

swirling gray ghosts

we forget

are made of water and wind,

until they hit us,
then hit us again.

***

But at least there's finally something to report this morning.

Florence starts as a red circle,
a path projected from Cape Verde's coast
through the expansive Atlantic.

    A tropical storm heading westward.

Florence sounds like the name
of a woman who wears floral perfume—
jasmine blooms wilting at her wrist.

A woman who keeps things neat,
but sometimes forgets to dust and sweep.

A woman who savors being the center of attention,
    who wears an orange shawl 'round her shoulders
    and enters every room with a big, *Hey, y'all!*

      Florence sounds like the type of woman
      for whom they'd name a storm.

***

I jot down notes on Florence
right before the bright bird chirps
of first bell twitter through the hall.

Before we can all file out,
Maria Reneé makes her way to the front door.

> She spreads her pageant voice thick
> as pimento cheese,
>   sweet as steeped tea.

> *Hold on,* she says.
> *I have an important announcement to make.*

She swings her glossy hair over her shoulder—
    a smooth, fluid movement fit for a stage.

We wait, impatient.

Ready for gossip or god knows what's
about to be dropped.

I look at Lola Sun—
        who looks at Todd—
            who turns to me,

                all of us braced
                with bated breath.

***

Maria Renée continues,
gestures as if we're judges to impress
instead of just her journalism friends.

> *As some of y'all already know,*
> *I've been super swamped lately*
> *with all these college apps.*
>
> *I don't want this process*
> *to affect the paper,*
> *so I've decided to choose*
>
> > *a second-in-command.*
>
> *I'll need someone creative and reliable.*
>
> > She shoots a glance at Maya,
> > then grazes her gaze over me.
> >
> > > *Someone,* she says, *who will follow directions,*
> > > *who won't step out of bounds.*

Shit, shit, shit.
> So she *did* hear about The Morning Minute.

Lola Sun Talks Me Out of a Temper Tantrum

My complaints rain over our Styrofoam lunch trays,
soggy and sloppy, high-pitched whines.

> *Maria Renée knows how badly I want this!*
> *One slip up doesn't mean*
> *I'm unteachable. In fact,*
> *it means I have vision and reach.*

> *And much as I love Maya,*
> *this opportunity doesn't matter to her as much.*

Past our mashed peas and terrible tapioca cups,
Lola Sun slides two things my way:

an exasperated look

and a note to unfold—
my name unfurled like ribbon
in cursive and gold ink.

Dear Capricorn,

Stop being so damn dramatic.
None of the personal planets are retrograde,
so any perceived conflict is self-made.

Ignore this impulse.

Next week, a new moon
will enter your ninth house—

> *now is the perfect time*
> *to turn plan into action.*

> *Publish. Teach. Take a trip.*

> *Push past where you presently stand.*

Lola Sun Also Has a Note for Garrett,

who's as much like an uncle to her as to me.

She asks me to hand it off
when I see him next.

> *Oh, Leo.*

> *You are in for a lot.*

> *Your sixth house is soon to be a full one*
> *with both Mars and Saturn stationed direct.*

> *This can lead to potential problems at work.*
> > *Pay attention.*
> > > *Be prepared.*

> *We often don't know where our limits lie*
> *until we've crossed that line.*

> *You're also in your Saturn Return.*
> *The planets are pushing you forward—*

> > *not with a gentle shove,*
> > *but with a forceful thrust.*

Even after Lunch with Lola Sun,

come evening, I'm teeming again
over Maria Renée's not-so-subtle implication.

Irritation tingles my skin,
a sticky heat—
> sweaty and heavy as humidity.

> Will this new second-in-command
> automatically become next year's editor?

> There's no way The Morning Minute
> cost me this opportunity.

> Another year of weather reports
> instead of front-page headlines.

I listen to Felicia Fitz's five o'clock slot
to fix my fuming.

Her polished and poised voice
runs through accidents and traffic patterns,

> reminds me I have a job to do.

I'm a journalist with a story to report,
even if it is just about a forming storm.

I won't go off script with this one—
I'll play it cool and follow the rules—

on the off chance I'm still viable
for second-in-command.

But maybe I can have a little fun with it.

I submit my weather report
straight to Stephen,
bypass all the usual edits.

Thursday, August 30th

The Bloom's Online Weather Report

Bonding features have now been identified in a tropical storm
  named Florence.
Under these conditions, the storm is likely to intensify.
Low air pressure
  and
Low wind shear
Strengthen storm bands and enable further organization.
High winds of sixty miles per hour have been reported.
It will still take several days to project the storm's course,
  but we'll be here
To cover it all.
    Visit our website for daily updates.

An Announcement's Made

Before Maria Renée even makes it
to the front office for The Morning Minute—

before my backpack is unzipped,

before Lola Sun can slip
what I suspect is a love letter—

or at least a like letter—

to Todd.

Principal Keys's voice reverberates over the intercom,
a little groggy,
an un-caffeinated froggy croak,

but his words hit clear and stern
as a hailstorm.

Millie Willard
to the principal's office.

Millie Willard
to the principal's office.

Principal Keys Lays It on Me Thick

Why is everything suddenly a joke to you, Miss Willard?
The Bloom is supposed to be serious student journalism.

Not prank drafts strung through with profanity.

Did you think no one would notice
BULLSHIT *spelled down the margin?*

I squirm in the faux-leather seat across from Keys.
The barometric pressure of the room
presses against my temples.
A migraine swims to the surface,
lights up as if I'm breathing
below sea level.

Keys continues: *I don't know*
who let this past proofreading,
but so help me
I am not above disbanding the paper altogether
if this type of behavior continues.

I protest Stephen's innocence
and Maria Renée's too—

tell him I was just trying to increase web traffic.

Detention, Miss Willard, he says,
straightening his checkered tie.

Detention and not another word.

A Fun Fact about Droughts

Droughts usually cause the most danger
in what disasters they pave the way for—
           famine, wildfires,
           complete deforestation.

The droughts are less the problem
than what will succeed them.

Kind of like how one stupid choice
      seems to loop into a stupid choice spiral,
      at least by all accounts of how my first week of school is going.

      First, I mouth off on The Morning Minute,
      and now this.

I'm not sure if I'm thick-skinned enough,
gritty or gutsy enough
      to make it through
      an afternoon of detention.

Each second the clock clicks by
is like the slow erosion
      of the soil in my mind.

      By second period, the rich red clay
      of my usual composure
          is cracked.

      By fourth, I'm desolate as a desert.

      Anxious and anticipating
      the worst.

Detention Is Comprised

solely of me and one other kid—

    a senior who spray-painted lunch trays
    as students ate off them—

        some alleged capstone project
        for a theater course.

For Keys to send us here,
he must be really pissed—
        his regular approach
        more prevention than punishment.

No matter how hard I try to focus
on fractions and Fibonacci,
my homework problems unfasten on the page.

Mama's gonna be in a rage
when she has to pick me up late—
        The Anchor's hosting a senators' summit tonight,
        and it's up to her to cook something scrumptious.

I can hear her now, hollering at the staff,
Someone make sure the cornbread don't burn
while I bust my delinquent daughter out of school.

Two seats away, spray-paint kid
mumbles monologues under his breath.

The lull of his speech
is almost soft and slow enough
to put me to sleep—

     until who walks in
     but the student I'd least suspect
     to ever be in detention:

          Maya Nickleson.

***

Maya blushes when she sees me,
explains herself in a rush of whispered words.

Millie! Hi! What are you doing here?

Me? Well, I'm not in trouble, you see.

She hands me her homework assignments.
Half-scribbles manic down the margins—
    entire problems struck through,
        faded ink where she's calculated and erased, calculated and erased.

I'm just already afraid of failing geometry.

She laughs nervously.

Sometimes I come in here,
use this space like study hall.

I've even had a tutor all summer.
I know it's only the first week of class,
but I had to take algebra twice to pass!

She shakes her head.
A few flakes of green glitter
fall free.

I know, I know, it's bad when
a photographer can't figure out angles.

We Spend Detention Shit-Talking

mostly about our math teacher,
Mr. Daldry, and how dumbfounding
his classes can be.

It's always so annoying, Maya says,
to ask a question in his class.

Literally every time a student says
"I don't understand,"

    he says, "Well, which part don't you understand?"

I clasp a hand over my mouth
to keep from laughing.

That's so true! I say.

    And it's like, if I knew
    what I didn't understand,
    I wouldn't have to ask, would I?

    I wouldn't embarrass myself
    in front of the whole class
    by raising my hand!

Maya snaps her fingers
in self-satisfied agreement.

Exactly!

I get so sick of his tired old shtick.

    "If you don't ask me the right questions,
    how can I help you find the right answers?"

Garrett Picks Me up from Detention in His Deputy Car

He lets the twang of a Hank Williams song
take up space for a few seconds
        while he decides
           between a good sheriff, bad sheriff approach
           as he drives me home.

He settles on good sheriff, says,

> *Looks like this Florence's fixin' to be worse*
> *than people think.*

> *I'm worried ain't enough townsfolk*
> *gonna take it serious—*
happens every season.

> *People peacock about staying and then wait too long,*
> *don't try to evacuate until it's too late.*

> *And I ain't talking about the elderly,*
> *or those who can't afford to go nowhere—*

> *Lord knows we'll do our best—*

> *but we don't have enough shelters in place*
> *to protect everyone who decides to stay.*

> *We're even considering Lindley Library—*
> *why, that building's almost a hundred years old!*

> *The outlets aren't grounded,*
> *the windows on the west side wall don't open,*
> *and the roof's not sloped right for rain drainage.*

We pull into my drive,
and I thank him for his time.

As I make to leave,
he reaches for my shoulder, says,

> *Don't let 'em make you feel too bad*
> *for a little misbehaving—*

> > *that's the Casey in you*
> > *to raise a little Cain.*

I smile and hand off
Lola Sun's note.

Post-Detention Dilemma

If Maria Renée knew about
Maya's trouble with geometry,

> she'd never choose her
> as second-in-command.

> > She wouldn't stand for someone
> > to potentially fail a math class
> > > in order to serve
> > the paper more.

But me, on the other hand,
my schedule's wide open.

> I have all the free time to offer
> if chosen—

> as long as I can manage
> to stay out of trouble's way.

This feels like scoring a story,
like soft investigatory reporting.

> Maya's geometry problems
> are the best lead I've had all week.

Friday, August 31st

Lola Sun Is Unimpressed

We sneak our lunches
to the bleachers—
    soak up some of summer's last sun.

        Thin wisps of clouds float by,
        too lazy to lay their shadows
        on the grass in passing.

I tell Lola Sun
about my meeting with Maya,
how poorly her time spent in tutoring
might be perceived by Maria Renée—

            when Lola Sun snaps on me,
            splits me dead center
            like a lick of lightning to an old oak tree.

I say, *But it's fate*
that made our paths cross!
If the stars didn't want me to know this—

            No, Millie, no, she says.

            Maya's problem in math class
            is not your story to tell.

            You don't help people by selling someone out,
            and you certainly don't blame it on the stars.

            The stars are many things
            but not an excuse to behave badly
            and call it "breaking news."

            Ambition isn't worth hurting others for,
            even if you are a Capricorn.

Saturday, September 1st

Mama Makes a Mean List of Chores as Post-Detention Punishment

Yard work and scrubbing floors,
laundry and dusting.

Tasks meant to break both my back
and this streak of bad behavior.

Two birds with one stone, Mama chirps—
                    storm prep and punishment.

                    I want my garden tarped,
                    my cast iron hand-scrubbed with salt, you hear?

                    And it better all be done
                    with a camera-ready smile,

                    or I'll go from Category One mad
                    to Category Five lickety-split.

That's not how storms work, I say.

                    It is in this house, Millie Willard,
                    Mama quips back. *It is in this house.*

Mama's Chores Aren't Half as Boring

once Lola Sun gets here to help.

Mama fries us hushpuppies and falafel for lunch,
then we go to scrub out the gutters.

> We gossip over the crunch
> of the leaves we clear out,

> talk newspaper shop as tacky black gunk
> gets stuck to our gloves.

> Two girls on two ladders, trying
> to keep our balance as we laugh.

Lola Sun pulls four polished stones
> from her pocket,
> > black gleam with a silver sheen.

> *Hematite*, she says,
> and places them in a line
> along the roof's rough shingles.

> *For grounding.*

> *I placed some under the porch too.*

> *They'll help your house*

> *ride out Florence.*

***

As Lola Sun finishes her grounding ritual,
whispers softly to the stones,

> a friendly greeting from behind
> makes me teeter in surprise.

> *Heard y'all might need some help.*

And here's Todd,
> power drill and thick-bristled paint brush in hand.

> Their hair now chopped in an asymmetrical bob,
> dyed a deep purple to match a Vikings jersey.

I look to Lola Sun,
> who holds my gaze for a moment,

> then blushes so deeply
> her faux-freckles pop,

> a natural shine on her cheeks—
> a highlight of sweat and giddiness,

> brighter than the sheen of her hematite.

Advice

Felicia Fitz said on the record once
that it takes strong skin to be a reporter.

That the best journalists never take anything personally.

Not when an interviewee is rude or crude
or catches an attitude.

Not when viewers write or call in
with scathing reviews,
when they criticize or question
your perspective.

And definitely not when competing stations
break a story first,
no matter how long or hard
you've worked.

I try my hardest to heed her advice, but

I bet Felicia's never felt the first stinging swirls
of a friend
slowly
slipping
away,
preferring
the closeness
of another person.

I like Todd and all,
but I like them more
when they're not vying to be
my best friend's love interest.

Todd Tries to Be Helpful,

but they're a little overzealous.

When Mama comes to meet them,
I pull Lola Sun aside.

> She says, *We're not officially dating,*
> *but we could be one day soon.*
>
> *Next week, maybe. Probably.*
>
> *I told Todd I wanted to hold off on being official*
> *until the next new moon for the freshest start.*
>
> *But we can all three hang out, right?*
> *It won't be weird?*

Her words are a rush
    of wayward wind,
        as if she's rehearsed them.

Suddenly, Mama screeches
    over the high whine
        of a struggling drill bit.

> *No, honey—no!*
> *Not yet!*

We rush to the house's back wall—
    the one with my bedroom window—

    to find Todd has drilled a piece of plywood
    over the panes, protection from the hurricane.

Mama tries hard to keep her voice
balanced on the tightrope between
        being polite
        and freaking out.

Honey, she says, *Thank you,*
but we didn't need that up yet.

Yeah, Todd, I bark.
What am I supposed to do now?

    Live for a week in the dark?

Tuesday, September 4th

Worried Whispers about Florence

finally start to flurry 'round town.

> It sticks to the streets,
> a verbal, panicked sleet freezing over.

Over the past few days, the storm's undergone
a period of rapid intensification,
> officially turned into a Category Four.

Now I would never root for a storm, *per se*,
but maybe I could see the world from its side.

> Between plastic and other pollutants,
> carbon emissions killing the coral reefs,
> corporations unable to keep our drinking water clean—

> > why, if I was the weather,
> > I'd want to make myself seen.

> Shit, even the little I have to deal with—

> > detention and best friend drama,
> > a hen-pecking Mama,

> > my dilemma over Maya
> > and whether she'll out-editor me—

> > > makes me want to surge

> > > > and surge

> > > > > and surge.

67

Rumor Has It

that a few news stations
will stay in town—
> local reporters who hope their stories
> will be called upon for national coverage.

They'll need a building large enough to house equipment—
multiple rooms they can soundproof for shooting.

> A place with back-up generators,
> close enough to the action,
> but re-enforced enough to be safe—

> a building the sheriff's office
> hasn't already secured as a shelter.

Rumor has it Felicia Fitz
and the Channel Five Crew
are considering their options,

> and the top spot
> is The Anchor.

> Mama's Anchor.

> My *in* to finally meet my favorite reporter.

Wednesday, September 5th

We Hold a Newspaper Roundtable

to discuss our options moving forward
    in the face of Florence.

Stephen—ever the straight-edge about deadlines—
    dreads the thought of a hiatus.

    He suggests, if school closes,
    we pre-upload content
    that he'll program to publish daily.

Maria Renée disagrees.

    It's a smart concept, Stephen,
    but I can't support it.

    Any material we pre-package now
    won't be relevant next week
    when the storm makes landfall.

    And what if people's power goes out?

    I don't want newsfeeds clogged
    with articles rushed out for clickbait.

    It'll be filler and The Bloom *readers*
    deserve, first and foremost, real news.

    If we wait, we wait,
    but it's the price we pay
    for precise reporting.

The Bloom's Online Weather Report

Current reports indicate Florence has now been downgraded
    to a tropical storm, torn
Apart by strong wind shear. This does not,
Unfortunately, put Magnolia in the clear.
Threat of landfall remains an issue as Florence could
Impact much of the Mid-Atlantic and Southeast
Once it regains hurricane strength.
Now is the time to take precaution and stock up on survival supplies.

I Ask Lola Sun to Read the Stars Again,

once Garrett leaves,
to see if there's any celestial comfort,

any galactic guidance they can provide
to him—the most social of all the signs.

She sends back:

> *Hello, Leo.*

> *Long time no read.*

> *As we discussed before,*
> *Saturn is stationed direct*
> *in your sixth house.*

> > *Prepare for more hours at work.*

> *Venus will venture into your tenth house—*
> *first forwards, then backwards*
> *in its dreamy retrograde.*

> *This is the realm of the domestic.*

> *Secure any nest eggs necessary.*

> *Appreciate your material possessions.*

Now is not the time
to take security for granted.

Then, to me:

Sorry, girl, I tried
to spin it positive,

but all I see
    is change
        in the forthcoming days.

The First Rains Come Sunday, Softly

Mama steeps rose hip tea,
its steam sweet.
        Bitter liquid
    a pale pink.

We each cup a mug
and snuggle on the couch.

        No homework today.
        No menu preparation
        or recipe testing.

We sit with each other in a silence
so warm and thick
you could stitch a quilt from it.

Mama touches up her red polish,
fills in the week's chips with swift brush flicks.

We are cradled in the gray haze
of a lazy afternoon.

Rain taps haphazard on the window,
and I fall into a comfy cat nap.

And Then Mama's Phone Rings,

a twinkling sound that stirs me
from dreams of reporting.

I can tell by how she straightens
her voice apron-string tight
that work's on the other line.

> *I see*, she says.
> *Yeah, I'm not sure.*

> *Overtime?*
> *Free lodging?*
> *For Millie too?*

> *I don't know,*
> *that's a lot of people to cook for,*
> *especially if the main power cuts out.*

> > *What about the wait staff?*
> > *My sous chef? What did they all say?*

I stir next to her.

> *Alright, let me think about it.*

She clicks her conversation off.

> *The Anchor thinks it's safer for us*
> *to weather the storm there.*

> *They want to impress*
> *all those news execs,*
> > *but I don't know, Millie.*
> > *I just don't know.*

I Consult My Vision Board

I ask for guidance from my journalist mentors.

How would Lisa Ling follow Florence?

What metrics would Rachel Maddow use
      to measure government preparedness
      as they track the path of a natural disaster?

My phone goes off.
      I expect a text from Lola Sun—
      she's here to pick me up for school—

      but what I see instead
      ignites spotlights within me,
      leaves me center-stage star-struck.

            It's a tweet from Felicia Fitz,
            confirmation that she
            and the Channel Five news crew

            will for sure cover the storm
            live from The Anchor.

***

All the way to school, I rattle my words off,
heavy as a rainstorm.

This is perfect! I practically scream.

Mama and I already have the offer to stay in town!

*I'll be able to report on Florence first-hand
and meet Felicia Fitz!*

My weather reports will be the best.

> *I'll impress Maria Renée,*
> *win the editorship on my own merit,*
> *and leave Maya with all the time she needs*
> *to grapple with geometry.*

It's perfect!

But Lola Sun is the spooky kind of silent as she drives,
the stillness of a hurricane's eye.

I want to say that's good news, Millie,
but I don't think people should stay.

*Todd says their family has nowhere else
near enough to go.*

I'm worried sick.

*I feel like a red dwarf star
swelling with nerves,*

hovering on the verge of implosion.

***

Principal Keys's voice is controlled yet curt
on The Morning Minute,

> a hint he's holding back
> administrative annoyances
> in the face of Florence prep.

>> *Dear students, be assured*
>> *that if absences are acquired*
>> *before we officially close on Thursday,*
>> *no students will be penalized.*

>> *Please pass this information on to your parents*
>> *so we can keep the office phone lines open.*

> A secretary snickers from somewhere behind him.

>> He closes out: *Student safety*
>>   *is our top priority.*

As We're Dismissed from Homeroom,

I head to Maria Renée's desk—

>   where multiple deadlines are drawn out,
>   projected timelines based on the different number
>   of school days we might miss.

>   *Maria Renée*, I say, *don't worry*
>   *about coverage on the ground.*

>   *My mom and I have a promising place to stay,*
>   *so just say the word!*

>   *Anything at all, you can count on me.*

Her eyes narrow as she considers
the cost of my offer—can she trust me
to deliver? Does this decision
make me more eligible for the editorship?

She softens, sighs.

>   *That's actually super helpful, Millie*, she says,
>   *because my parents want to leave—and soon.*

Mama Makes an Announcement

Pack your bags, Millie, she says
as soon as I'm home from school.
We're leaving in the morning.

> *Wait, what?* I ask.

The soft waft of cinnamon floats from the kitchen—
an attack.
> Mama's baked oatmeal cookies,
> a peace offering for after
> the battle she's about to wage.

> *We can't leave, Mama!*
> *I already promised Maria Renée!*
> *I need to meet Felicia Fitz!*
> *Staying at The Anchor is the perfect plan!*

Mama pinches the bridge of her noise
as if she's smelt the earthy burp of spoiled spinach.

Honey, she says,
Garrett's serious about us leaving.
He's afraid the highway will be too congested by Thursday,
and I'm afraid we could be stuck during a flash flood.

I'm shouting now.

> *I can't believe you!*
> *You're going to crush my career,*
> *stall it out before it ever starts!*
> *All you care about is yourself*
> *and your dumb restaurant.*

79

I sound absurd even to myself,
but anger surges through me,
too hot to stop.

I clench my fists
the same way certain plants curl their leaves
to shrink size during storms,
reduce the risk of being blown away.

Millie, you're sixteen.
And once Maria Renée graduates—
I mean, that's only four months
plus four months from now—

I stomp away, slam my bedroom door.

You hear that, Casey?
Mama asks Daddy's framed portrait
which hangs above the fireplace.

Your daughter's mad at me
because I won't let her stay in town and drown.

Things a Hurricane Stirs up before It Arrives

Whispered warnings of the wind,
sordid as a storm surge,
as swamp water churning.

The humming scent of honeysuckle,
sweet and hurried on the breeze.

A symphony of stress from household pets—
    cats scratching against couch cushions,
    birds chirping during the dark of night.

Anxiety among family members and friends,

    fraught with the thought of evacuation,

      their fears slick and twisted,

        exposed as the tangled root systems of trees
        blown past their tipping points.

Lola Sun Stops by in the Morning

to say goodbye before we drive away.

Once school finishes on Thursday,
her family will leave.

Trying not to cry stings
like rubbing the underside
of a nettle leaf across my eyes,
so we hug—tightly in silence.

She slides a bright blue stone
veined with whispers of gold
into my pocket.

Turquoise, she says.

    For the storm? I ask.

She shakes her head.

So you'll find your voice,
and it won't falter.

Via Texts, We Share Our Exit Strategies

Maria Renée's family is also leaving today,
heading toward Savannah to stay with an aunt.

Maya and Lola Sun will both depart Thursday
straight after school,
      right when it's predicted
      the sky will unspool itself
    into gray welts of weather.

Stephen's family will stay,
but their house is settled
on a steep incline—
    designed specifically
    to stand outside
    bad weather's wingspan.

    Stephen invited Todd and their family
    to stay in the spare guestrooms,
    much to Lola Sun's relief.

And here I am, bags packed—

    all our important documents and pictures
    wrapped in plastic—

slamming the trunk shut,

    trying in vain
    not to huff at Mama

      as we buckle up,
      as the ignition twitches on.

We Pull out of the Driveway

Mama sighs, and I try not to
let her hear me cry
from the passenger seat.

    She places her hand on my knee,
    but I turn to face my window.

        I can't let go of feeling
        like this is a mistake.

            Staying at The Anchor
            makes a much better story

            than a boring pilgrimage
            to small, sleepy Ninth Tree.

A glint of sunlight strikes
the silver-black stones Lola Sun left on the roof.

Stay safe, I think
as we drive away—

    from our house and hometown,
    from our family and friends,

        from what would have been
        a perfect journalistic opportunity,

            from Florence and who knows what
            destruction she'll bring.

11. Florence

Our Drive Is Six Hours of Silence

It simmers, sautés into a sour heat
between the driver and passenger seat.

Mama's mood worsens
because Garrett's prediction
proves true—
        early storm-evaders
 swarm the roads.

        We can barely inch forward
      without the fear of rear-ending someone's bumper.

The rain makes it worse.
Massive drops drive into the windshield,
     wipers waving frantically to keep up.

Mama's hands look so inept
at the steering wheel—white-knuckled,
shaky.
     So unlike the fluid fingers
     and quick wrist slips
     required of her fancy knife skills.

We stall right before
the state line—
       one small car stuck
     in evacuation traffic.

I wonder if Mama is nervous
over the memory of Daddy's accident.

If he could falter—skilled as he was,
slide out of control on the hairpin turn's sharp curve—

    how much worse are the odds of getting hurt
    with people crowded out here,
    honking at each other like pissed-off geese?

For Mama's sake,
I better buck up now,
        best as I can.

Ninth Tree, North Carolina

is a town of around four thousand.

Best known to tourists for its barbeque—
                slow-roasted pig shoulder
          and golden mustard sauce,
      served with a side of slaw.

Mama says no chef who cares about their customers
would clog their arteries with animal fat,

     but Ellis and Thayer say
     they'd eat that shit seven days a week
     if the joint didn't close on Sundays.

We pull into their drive.
     How long will this be our home?
        Two days? Four, tops?
I'm trading in my first-hand Florence action
     for three adults squabbling
     over whether jackfruit
     is a good pork substitute.

I'd roll my eyes straight up to the sky
if that didn't mean I'd see the storm.

In Middle School, We Played M.A.S.H.

Mansion, apartment, shack, house.

> Someone drew a spiral, counted its lines—
> how many times it wound around itself—
> and counted off options for possible life paths.

> Mansion, apartment, shack, house.

Thayer and Ellis must have made some magic spirals
to pull off living here.

A huge two-story brick studio—
> the building attached
> adjacent to the fire station.

Open concept, flooded with light.
> White walls and hanging baskets of broad-leafed plants.

> A seven-foot-by-seven-foot square of wall art,
> stitched from red and gold yarn—
> > courtesy of one of Ellis's more famous real estate clients.

Mama and I are directed to the guest bedroom,
a queen with a quilt of colorful birds.

> A box of chocolates near the pillow
> and the half-hidden paws of Jasper,

> > Ellis's old and ornery tabby cat.

Ellis's Skin Is Warm and Dark,

like polished stromalite—
        his personality steady
        as rainstorms that arrive
        when predicted.

    He wears his hair cropped close,
    the waft of some expensive cologne
    a second shadow behind him—
        ginger and myrrh and musk.

    He's been friends with Mama since college,
    when she reimagined microwave dinners
    with spices and sauces in their communal student lounge.

Thayer has the pale pink finish
of sunstone—the parts that don't burn orange
when flashed with light.

    He breezes in and out of rooms
        like a wind worried it'll run out of time,
            frenzied to pollinate just one flower more,
                to serve as undercurrent for some fresh-winged bird.

    He collects colorful socks and coffee pots,
    teaches sociology at the community college.

Mama worries about them here—
a biracial gay couple in a small Southern town.

I ask where they should go instead,
prejudice and its dreadful presence
able to wield its ugly head anywhere.

Mama clicks her tongue.

> *Sure, there's hatred everywhere, Millie,*
> *but still—some places are more a safe haven*
> *than others.*

> *I'm just grateful*
> *they've agreed to be ours.*

Mama Melts Chocolate on the Stove,

heats cream. Sprinkles a pinch
of cinnamon on top.

This isn't vegan, I say.

> *It's not for me*, she shushes
> and hands Ellis a mug.

> *A little dairy is a small price to pay*
> *to make a friend his favorite drink.*

All night the adults catch up on the couch.
I half listen—
> my attention more attuned
> to Lola Sun's texts.

> I write, *What can you tell me*
> *about an Aries/Leo match?*

> *Ah!* She writes back.
> *Fire with friendly fire!*

> *These two fuel each other.*

> *Leo is the startling orange spark of ignition,*
> *while Aries is the high-temperature blue center of a flame.*

> *It's heat that binds these two together.*

When I read this to the guys, Ellis laughs,
a thin chocolate foam mustache above his lip.

> *Leave it to you, Heather Grace*, he quips,
> *to have made such a weird one.*

Wednesday, September 12th

Quiet Cobwebs Itself over Every Empty Space

as we ready ourselves for the storm this morning.

Mama reads cookbooks to calm her nerves;

Thayer grades papers in the kitchen;

Ellis posts listings on his phone,
though business the next few weeks
will be nonexistent.

It's an uneasy quiet—
one that settles like dust,
feels like it needs to be swept up.

A silence with lips pursed,
on the verge of whispering

Florence

Florence

Florence.

93

Everything from the Window's View Is Distorted by Rain

The barbecue diner and local pizza joint that stand across the street
are now barely-there squares of brick,
    visible only through a slanted-eye squint.

The stoplight at the crossroads—
    hardly a faint gold halo
    to slow drivers down.

Forget about seeing the trees
through these sideways sheets of water—
    the thickest, darkest trunks
    materialize then melt,
        soaked to the bone,
        floating in and out of sight like ghosts.

Even my own face, reflected back to me
in the windowpane,
        is luminous and distorted,
    similar yet strange—

    the way I sometimes see Mama's eyes
        or Daddy's smile

    staring in the mirror back at me.

After Supper, Thayer Suggests a Game

Millie, he says,
you can't keep watching
storm coverage—you'll go cross-eyed.

>   *And, Heather Grace, you're gonna bake*
>   *me out of house and home*
>   *if you don't leave my dry goods pantry alone.*

>   *C'mon, now, both of you.*

We play a few rounds of Kemps—
>   Mama and I search for any sign
>   the men might be sliding each other under the table.

They win hand after hand,
again and again—
>   so subtle is their signal.

Finally, after their fifth win—

>   it hits me!

Jasper!

The nasty-tempered cat hisses
as I reach to scratch its back.

They pet Jasper
every time they have a winning hand!

Ellis throws down his cards
but makes no denial,
>   and Thayer's smile
>   betrays their defeat.

***

As I brush my teeth, get ready for sleep,
    Mama screeches from the living room—

    urgent weather updates stream on the TV.

    Ninth Tree's local channel
    has nothing on Felicia Fitz,
    but it'll suffice for now.

Mama cheers over the announcement—

    She's downgraded!

    She's downgraded!

    Florence is only a Category One!

She hugs me in relief—
    her scent a comforting blend of vanilla and sweat—
but we both know *only* isn't quite the right word.

Florence Hits

With winds whirling
at ninety miles an hour,
she carves herself haggard and hard
into the coast of Wrightsville Beach, North Carolina,
    three hours from where we are now,
        but only eighty miles
        from our home.

The storm itself is slow,
takes its sweet time to terrorize
those trapped in its path.

At a crawl of five miles an hour,
Florence could unleash hundreds—
if not thousands—of gallons of rain
over the towns she surges through.

What we now must fear most
        is floodwaters.

The Bloom's Unofficial Weather Report

rain rain rain rain rain rain rain rain rain rain rain rain rain
rain rain rain rain rain rain rain rain rain rain rain rain rain
rain rain rain rain rain rain rain rain rain rain rain rain rain
rain rain rain rain rain rain rain rain hail rain rain rain rain
rain rain rain rain rain rain rain rain rain rain rain rain rain
rain rain rain rain rain rain rain rain rain rain rain rain rain
rain rain rain rain ~~gusts of wind~~ rain rain rain rain rain
rain rain rain rain rain rain rain rain rain rain rain rain rain
rain rain rain rain rain rain rain rain rain rain rain rain rain
rain rain rain rain rain rain rain rain rain rain rain rain rain
rain rain rain rain rain rain rain rain rain rain rain rain rain
rain rain rain rain rain rain rain rain rain rain rain rain **l** rain
rain rain rain rain rain rain rain rain rain rain rain rain rain
rain rain rain hail rain rain rain rain rain rain rain rain **i** rain
rain rain rain rain rain rain rain rain rain rain rain rain rain
rain rain rain rain rain rain rain rain rain rain rain rain **g** rain
rain rain rain rain rain rain rain rain hail rain rain rain rain
rain rain rain rain rain rain rain rain rain rain rain rain **h** rain
rain rain rain rain rain rain rain rain rain rain rain rain rain
rain rain rain rain rain rain rain rain rain rain rain rain **t** rain
rain rain rain rain rain rain rain rain rain rain rain rain rain rain
rain rain rain rain ^{stormsurge} rain rain rain rain rain rain rain **n** rain
rain rain rain rain rain rain rain rain rain rain rain rain rain
rain rain rain rain rain rain rain rain rain rain rain rain **i** rain
rain rain rain rain rain rain rain rain rain rain rain rain rain
rain rain rain rain rain rain rain rain rain rain rain rain **n** rain
rain rain rain rain rain rain rain rain rain rain rain rain rain rain
rain rain rain rain rain rain rain rain rain rain rain rain **g** rain
rain rain rain rain rain rain rain rain rain rain rain rain rain[1]

---

1   Three-hundred thousand North Carolina homes and four-thousand South
     Carolina homes have lost power. Anticipate prolonged outages.

I Wake to Horns

Barely audible over the roar
of relentless rain, the steel screech of large machines
   maneuver to a stop.

Slowly, so as not to wake Mama
on the bed's other side,
   I glide curious across the living room,
   peer outside.

Gray-green tanks park in the adjacent firehouse lot—
  members of the National Guard.

Service men and women unload rescue boats,
debrief with the local fire chief.

Their presence both calms and unnerves me.
We're safer because they're close,

  but those rescue boats might mean
  there are locals trapped nearby,

    crawling to attics and on top of roofs

      just to stay afloat.

I Livestream Channel Five on Mama's Laptop

Felicia Fitz's olive raincoat,
    whipped so hard by the wind

        it looks like it's wrapped itself around her tiny frame twice.

Subtitles are needed
because there's no understanding
the sound of her words over the storm.

A photo montage flashes—
    submerged houses,
    trees blown onto roads.

                I freeze
                the frame

                as one picture
                sickens me to the quick.

                    Mama, I call, *The Anchor!*

                    The Anchor's underwater!

***

The hotel's first floor appears flooded—
    a person on the street knee-deep in standing water,
    a seasick shade of green.

A fire hydrant is almost completely submerged,
    its red rounded tip barely visible
    over the water's surface.

Well, I'll be damned, Mama whispers.
See, baby, I told you
    it wasn't a safe place to stay.

But the longer I look,
the more messed up the picture's proportions become.

    It's distorted.

    The water should lay straight across all planes—
        instead, it slants
            toward the photograph.

Maya's talked about this before—
how half a picture is perspective.

Oh, dear Lord, I say,
Mama—it's just the angle.
Look!

I tilt the screen sideways
and we see the truth—

    the water's nowhere near as high
    as The Anchor's first floor.

    The image *is* an illusion.

***

Mama goes off like a fire alarm
over burning bacon grease.

> *They should be ashamed!*
> *All of us who evacuated*
> *need a clear sense*
> *of what wreckage we'll return to,*
>
> > *and they're peddling spoof pictures—*
> > *cheap gimmicks and tricks!*

Mama has a point, but she doesn't know
how hard photojournalists work
to have their images shown.

> *Yeah, it might be shady,*
> *but they get paid for clickbait.*

Mama won't hear none of it, though.
She dismisses my defense.

> *What will matter most four months past Florence,*
> she says, *is how helpful news reporters were,*
>
> *is if they kept people safe.*
>
> *It won't matter one damn*
> *about tricky tactics to drive website traffic*
>
> *if they spread misinformation.*
>
> > *Channel Five should be ashamed.*
> >
> > *And you should be too, Millie,*
> > *if you support this.*

We Don't Speak for the Rest of the Day

Mama thinks I'm asleep now,
    but I hear her at the kitchen sink,
    washing out thin-stemmed cocktail glasses.

They all started in on rosemary spritzers in the early afternoon—
    little left to do at that point
    except day-drink as a distraction

        from the lights flickering on and off,
        from the wind-swept debris striking the windows.

Mama starts in on a long laundry list of concerns,
stringing an invisible clothesline
    from Ellis's ears to Thayer's.

Our house isn't paid off.

    What happens if there's water damage?
    If a tree falls on the roof?

    The hotel hasn't even confirmed
    if they'll cover our missed days at work.

        I don't know how far my savings will stretch
        in lieu of steady paychecks.

    And then there's Millie—
    she's gotten in so much trouble at school lately.

    I don't know
    when she got so hard-headed.

I snuggle further underneath the covers,
will the rain to grow louder.

Texts from Lola Sun

Your mom's a Virgo, Millie.
Loss of control is hard for her.

Try not to take it to heart.

We All Check in via Texts

Maria Renée's missed the worst of it in Savannah
thanks to the storm's southward shift.

> She's stir-crazy in her *tia*'s house,
> but at least she's being fed fresh *mofongo*.

Lola Sun lost power last night.

Maya, this morning.

> She plays shadow puppets
> to appease her niece
> with whatever muddled-colored sun
> makes it through their window.

And Stephen and Todd make the time
sound like one big sleepover—

> besides the terrifying thunder,

> > the pine tree that splintered,
> > its branch catching the corner of Stephen's roof,
> > scratching off a handful of shingles.

They volunteer to drive by everyone's house
for damage assessment
once the roads are cleared from debris,

> > which is reassuring,
> > except no one knows
> > how much longer
> > that might be.

***

Once everyone's certified themselves as safe,
Maria Renée starts in on one of her pageant speeches.

> *And did y'all hear what the President said?*
> *He had the nerve to travel to North Carolina and say,*
> > "The wettest we've ever seen
> > from the standpoint of water."

WHAT DOES THAT EVEN MEAN?!?!?!?!

Maya sends a string of emoji skulls.

Wish we could've been there to protest!

Stephen texts:

> *In this weather, are you kidding?*
> *There isn't a raincoat thick enough.*

I sense the unspoken eye-rolls
behind the screen of every phone in this convo—

> and I'm grateful for my friends
> and their funny banter,

> > even as the storm scatters us
> > across three different states.

***

Our texts remind me of a crucial concern,
    a timeline that's escaped me since evacuation,
    its ticking down drowned out by Florence.

By semester's end, Maria Renée
will still need to appoint an editorial assistant,

    and what have I done yet
    to deserve that title,
    to be worthy of a byline
    better than weatherwoman?

Outside our window,
the National Guard loads supplies
into tarped-roofed tanks,
    their eyes tired,
    their camouflage less crisp
    than when they first arrived.

An idea begins to circulate,
    like a wind itching to be wayward.

I Sneak Downstairs, past All the Adults

Mama bakes banana bread for breakfast—
wrapped up in small kitchen distractions
to stave off her cooped-up and uncertain nervousness.

In one hand, my phone—its voice memo app pulled up.
In the other, my umbrella.

I exit the garage door
and walk to the rain-soaked parking lot.

    No one the wiser
    except Jasper,
    who hides beneath the stairs.

        He twitches his whiskers,
        lets out a hiss

           as I close the door
           and the wet wind hits him.

***

No one lets me get a word in edgewise
as I wedge myself between the tanks
    and boxes of food bank donations
    they're hauling on deck.

Still, I hold my phone close enough
to record any responses.

    Hi, Millie Willard here,
    reporting for The Bloom.

    Can you confirm that the storm
    has left at least twelve dead?

    How have state and federal disaster funds
    been allocated so far?

        A fatigue-furrowed man
        finally casts a glance my way.

        Kid, how old are you—thirteen?
        Go back inside. We have work to do.

Sir, I say,
so do I.

***

A woman with wide, kind eyes
agrees to be interviewed
    on the condition I go back inside
    once I have what I need.

I ask her what's the worst she's seen so far.

    She says, *It's the small things*
    that upset you.

        Not the floodwaters—
        those don't hit you first.
        Huge waves that seem some sort of Hollywood fake.
        Too surreal to be taken seriously.

    It's the small things.
    The three white wooden crosses
    floating around I-95 near the Fayetteville exit—
        memorials clean tore up from the ground.

    It's how we rescued an old woman down the road
    who didn't want to abandon the home
    her husband died in,
        the hem of her floral night gown soaked.

    How my own grandmother
    recalled Hurricane Hazel
    back when she was a girl.

        How easily we pretend stories are just that—

        that all our worst storms have already passed.

***

I take the woman's name and rank,
    thank her for her time,
        save the recording,

          and then my grip slips—
          fingers slick with rain.

        I watch

           my phone

         fall,

              strike

                  the sidewalk,

                        s h a t t e r.

The glass cracks into a million fractures—
red pixelated lines pulse across the screen

    like the spaghetti maps
    that originally projected Florence's path.

      With a sharp, static crackle,
      the phone short-circuits,

flashes one final time,
fades to black.

I Could Report

on how Mama's voice is loud and sour,
shouting about how irresponsible I am.

> *A broken phone when a hurricane's*
> *driven us from our home!*

> *What if there's an emergency?*
> *Oh, that's right—*
> > *it IS an emergency, Millie!*

I could make note of the soft,
placated faces of Ellis and Thayer,
> who clearly don't want to take sides,
> their silence humid and humming.

I could document the sickness
in my stomach—a wash of acid,
a raw uprooting.

> I won't be able to reach
> Lola Sun or anyone.

But the worst part is how,
> for the first time ever,

> this embarrassment
> makes me feel like
> > being a reporter
> > might not be
> > worth
> > the
> > fight.

Garrett FaceTimes Us on Mama's Phone—

a frenzied flush to his skin,
his cheeks severely sunken in.

It's bad here, Heather Grace, he says.

Shifting high-pitched voices drift
from the dark rooms behind him.

Ear-splitting dog barks erupt
among rows of bookshelves,
cots scraped across the linoleum floor.

Lindley Library was designated to be the pet-friendly shelter,
and I drew the short end of the stick.

Been stationed here since Friday,
what with the fleas and ticks and piss.

And those damn windows don't open,
so it feels like we're all just fumigating
in the scent of feces and sweat.

Not to mention this hard-headed librarian staff.
As state employees, they're mandated to stay,
to help run the shelter.
            And they ain't pleased.

This one woman, she don't listen worth two shits,
don't have a lick of common sense.
She's pissed she's here and takes it out
by flat-out ignoring her assigned tasks.

    If I didn't know any better,
    I'd say she doesn't care if we live or die,

        that she's stationed herself
        firmly on the storm's side.

After Two More Days, the Rain Stops—

but the rivers don't.

They rise like hands in church,
water hungry to be seen in worship.

Black River, Lumber, Cape Fear.

Mama hardly speaks to me.
        She turns up her nose
        like I reek of burned Brussels sprouts,
        like garlic turned sour on the stove.

I don't dare ask to borrow her phone, so,
        for all I know,
        Lola Sun could be flooded
        out of house and home.

        She lost power two days ago,
        not even a charged computer
        on which to send a message.

                She could be stranded in her attic,
                awaiting rescue.

To ease this tension—

        the four of us suffocated
        like sous-vide vegetables
        sealed in an air-tight plastic pouch—

                Thayer suggests we get off the couch,
                take a walk outside.

It's Hard to Breathe in This Humidity

Sweat sticky on my forehead and neck
in the first few seconds.

Usually after a rain, the world
    looks rinsed and regal—

        trees more freshly green,
        an emerald sheen to the grass.

But everything is gray now—

        the sidewalk where a whole concrete block
        has been upturned by the churning wind,

        the barbecue joint's broken windowpane,
        shattered glass and baking sheets
            blown out onto the street.

Even the trees seem gray,
    like their black-brown bark's been stripped,
    exposing the lighter-colored bones beneath.
    The streets here are lined with pines,
    their names prettier than any palms
    we have back home—
        loblolly, ponderosa—

        but our Sabals are studier,
        the leaves and roots of our needle palms
        more likely to hold on tight
        during the fright of a storm like Florence.

Look, I say, pointing
to a fragile, forlorn pine,
that broken branch
looks like a fishing pole!

> *I think it is*, Thayer says,
> squinting for a sharper view.

And we're right.

> Some poor fisherman's pole
> hangs broken from a branch,

> swings twenty feet up—

>> its bright orange bobber
>> electric against the sky,

>>> the one bit of color
>>> the world's brave enough to muster.

Thursday, September 20th

I'm Jostled Awake—

Mama shakes my shoulders vigorously,
as if she's shifting flour.

Hurry, Millie—we're heading home.

  Why? What's going on? I ask.

  My sleep-thick speech
  sits ticklish in my throat.

*Someone posted a route
of roads open to Magnolia.*

*No clear interstates yet,
but apparently there's a backwoods path.*

  *Mama, I say, the governor warned last night—
  don't travel unless you must.*

*Millie, if we don't leave now—
who knows when the roads will be open again?*

C'mon and get up.

Your bags are packed.

Ellis Gives Me Departing Gifts

He tries to persuade Mama to stay
for a few more days,

    but she's frantic
    as a popcorn kernel
    in a pan of oil.

Realizing he can't change her mind,
he hands me a shoebox.

    Here, take this. Not sure how it wound up with us,
    but it's a box of Casey's belongings.

    He then sneaks me off to the side
    as Mama finishes loading the minivan,
    slips me a hundred-dollar bill.

    Get that phone fixed, he says,
    and keep recording stories.

***

It's inaccurate to say the drive back
takes us through a ghost town.

    True, there's not a soul around,
    no traffic passing through.

But everything's too wet to be dead—
    like a body sweating out a fever,
    blisters ruptured to blood and pus.

We make it thirty miles
toward I-95—

    have to loop through twice on the side roads
    suggested in that social media post.

We drive slow but smooth,
    and just when I start to think

        we might make it back home,
        I shout,

        Mama, watch out!

***

From the road perpendicular to us,
a wall of water rushes—

 a foot of risen rivers—

  storm surge sweeps straight for us.

  White-capped crests crash forward
  with sick gurgles and grunts.

Millie! Mama cries,
eyes wide as wreckage.

I grasp my seat
 as the water hits the car's side—

 impact, the surprise
 of its strength and suddenness.

  My shoulder hits the side door,
  immediately slumps slack and sore.

Water slides underneath our tires.

 We tilt.

  We sway.

Millie! Mama screams.

  We're about
  to be carried

   away.

It Should Be Loud Now,

but all I can hear

is Mama's

breath.

Each

exhale

a

prayer.

A

protection

spell.

***

Moments later, the water recedes,
swept off to the road's other shoulder.

Everything looks the same as it did before
        besides the oil-slick shine
        the water's left behind—

                a green-pink shift on black tar.

                Mama, I say,
                turn off the car.

                We don't want the engine to rust.

But Mama's on the road's shoulder,
doubled-over—

        the wet, wretched sounds
        of throwing up.

***

Mama heaves, hiccups,
    hyperventilates in waves of shaky breaths.

    Her inhales rapid and shallow,
    like worry's wrapped its worn hands
    around her lungs, suffocating her from inside out.

Garrett said Mama used to have
bad panic attacks after Daddy died—

    an elevated heart rate,
    a flash of heat,

      long crying spells
      that left her nauseous and numb—

but I've never seen one
    and don't know how to help.

I run out of the car to be by her side,
    cup her clammy hands in mine.

    Whisper over and over,

      It's okay, Mama. We're gonna be okay.

      Not knowing if it's true.

***

Once Mama's recovered enough,
she pops the hood,
    assesses potential damage—
    what the water might later
    rust or corrode.

We can probably make it back to Ninth Tree,
but you'll have to drive, Millie.

I can't risk another panic attack
on the road.

    Don't worry, honey,
    you have your permit.
    You know enough
    to know what to do.

I nod, climb into the driver's seat—
    the steering wheel firm
    beneath my curved fingers.
    The van seems so much bigger now.

And then I cry.

I can't, Mama. I can't!

I'm too scared.

I'm sorry about school and my phone and—

Mama scoots me into her lap.

Oh, Millie, she says
into the humid jungle of my hair.

We sit there as I cry
into the soft heap of her chest,

her body heat,

her ragged heartbeat.

We Make It Back to Ninth Tree

Thayer doesn't say much,
just hugs us and hums
    a soft, nervous tune.

Ellis runs his hands
up and down my arms—

    as if to warm them,
    as if to be assured we're really back
    in one piece.

I excuse myself to shower,
    to scrub the sour stench of fearful sweat
    off my exhausted body.

And Mama retreats back to the guest room
to cry again.

    It's a lazy metaphor
    to compare her tears to the rain,

      but it's all I've seen for days.

Even More Bad News

Mama avoids the news,
but I livestream Channel Five.

    Yes, it's still hurricane feed,
    but the headlines distract me
    from how detached Mama's become,
        how worn down and withdrawn.

BREAKING NEWS

streams across the screen
on a bright blue banner.

Felicia Fitz sits up straight
at a familiar desk—
    The Anchor's reception room.

    We can now confirm
    the fire that erupted
    from the west gallery
    of Lindley Library
    has been contained.

    We are trying to get confirmation now
    on whether local law enforcement officers
    and citizens were able to get out.

Flames unfold like a mountain range.
White gold heat-capped
in an array of electric orange crests.

Billows of black smoke.
Half the building ablaze.

Felicia continues:

No information yet
on injuries or deaths.

Mama, I call out—

That's where Garrett is!

***

Garrett's unreachable by his personal phone.

　　All we receive are the bleak,
　　disappointing beeps
　　of his dial tone.

　　Even the sheriff's office is swamped—
　　　　pre-recorded voicemails
　　　　　　staticky and asking us to leave a message.

That's it! Ellis says,
after our fifth attempt
to get through fails.

　　No more worrying over what'll have to wait.
　　Garrett will be fine, I promise.

Mama's eyes are red and wide.
What if we lose a family member to Florence?

　　Heather Grace, Ellis says, *let's start on dinner.*

He and Mama rummage in the cupboards.

　　It's gonna be a stone-soup type of supper,
　　our dry goods supply running low.

After Supper,

we sleuth through Daddy's shoebox—
    mostly old newspaper scraps,
    some sun-faded family photos.

    That's funny, Mama says,
    I don't remember none of this.

    We found it cleaning out
    the guest closet, Thayer says.

What stands out most to me
is a stiff stack of crackled weather reports—
    Daddy's notes scribbled on the side
    of each day's forecast.

    Wrong, he wrote on a day projected to be cloudy.
    I wanted that coverage to draw out the trout—
    ain't no fish swimming as the shallows warm.

    Wrong again, written
    on a Saturday forecasted to be sunny.

    Spent all morning
    in this damn deer stand
    riding out a thunderstorm.

Mama scoffs,
leafs through them gently.

    Must've been before I cut him off
    from eating meat.

Ellis smirks, says,

    Unless he was hiding it from you.
    He was a hen-pecked husband, Heather Grace.

She rolls her eyes, and we laugh—
    Daddy's past chagrins with local weathermen
    lift our spirits before sleep.

    I wish he were here now to write an alternate ending—
    to correct the past month's coverage.

    It's all a lie, he'd write. *Didn't no hurricane sweep through*
       our streets.

      No buildings destroyed.
       No roads demolished.
         Ain't no one get hurt.

III. One Week Past Florence

Saturday, September 22nd

We Leave Today—

the governor finally granted
the go-ahead to drive home.

Most main roads have been cleared,
most water has returned to its rivers.

We're too scared to be sad.
We depart with heavy doubt,
the weight of which doubles down on itself.

As I close the passenger door,
I brush my new bruise—
a yellow-purple sphere
of mottled shoulder.

It looks like ametrine,
like one of Lola Sun's stones.

How I wish she were here now
to map out our star charts
so we'd know what to expect
when we reach home.

Did her hematite help our house stand strong,
or did it backfire into a hex?

What if there's nothing left
but ruin and wreckage?

I finger the turquoise she gave me
less than two weeks ago—

how she promised me,

no matter what,

I'd find my voice.

At the City Limits

WELCOME
TO MAGNOLIA

The five-foot wide, vinyl-coated sign
       located right outside city limits

   has been shredded in the storm,
   one side torn off completely,

its remaining language
shorn straight through the middle.

All that's visible on the fabric
flapping in the wind is

ELC
TO MAGN

With what's left of the barely-there billboard,
I Bananagrams the surviving letters—
   try to read some message in the wreckage.

   gelato c'mn

   lc montage

   Camelot-ng

   tangle.com

Nothing works.

There is no hope or encouragement
in the remaining words—
      just a billboard,
      rain-battered and torn.

A Single Gas Station in Town Is Open

They ration out one red canister per family.

We wait behind a line of people on foot—
    people whose cars presumably won't start,
        already drained or left stranded in the storm.

Most people must not
have running water—
    unshowered hair hangs slack on shoulders,
    tied into sweaty top knots.

Most people must not
have working AC yet—
    tank tops and cutoff jeans,
    hands flapping like fans by their faces.

Most must be
strapped for cash—
    a man barters a watch for the gas can,
    is given it for free and waved on.

We get ours, grateful
we arrived before they ran out—

    otherwise, we'd be stranded too,

        without a prayer or backup plan.

This Is Not Brave to Admit

Not the behavior of a true reporter,

    but as we creep up to our driveway,

        I'm so taken with the fear
        of what we'll find—

           I close my eyes.

***

Mama starts to cry
in the driver's seat—

    there's such a thin line
    between the guttural sounds of grief

      and the soft sobs of relief.

        Eyes closed,
          I can't tell
            which side
              of the line
                we've arrived on.

Bless Lola Sun and Her Shiny Pebbles of Protection!

Our house is still standing!

      Mama and I clasp each other in happiness.
    No water rushing beneath us,
no storm surge about to sideswipe our car,

      just a family finally able to come back home.

An Initial Assessment of the Damage

Stripped shingles are scattered
across the backyard—
    shiny and black in the sun,

        like some blackbird of mythical proportion molted,
    shed feathers as it flew overhead.

Our front door is warped—
absorbed too much water
and expanded in its frame.

And one corner of the living room ceiling
has leaked—
    the wood floor beneath water-logged,
    the ceiling's plaster a Rorschach blot
            of swamp colors.

But our home is mostly okay—
    no real structural damage to speak of,
    no valuables misplaced or destroyed.

        Not even a broken windowpane
        thanks to the plywood
        Todd helped us fasten and secure.

        Even Mama's stained glass window pane
        is perfectly preserved.

           Its orange and blue squares
           still here to color her hands as she chops.

Lola Sun Brings Back a Level of Shine

the storm stripped from my life.

> She's back home too,
> but her power's not on.

No faux freckles painted on her face today,
no heart-shaped red frames.

> She's on my front porch in a faded gray t-shirt,
> top knot twisted sideways on her head.

You look like shit, I say,
as we laugh-cry in exhaustion and relief.

Without Lola Sun,
> I'm a chunk of rough quartz
> that has yet to be cut.

> Her laughter facets me
> with the right angles
> for light to pass through.

***

We lounge around,
    paint Mama's waitress red polish
        precisely on our nails.

       We blow on them dramatically
       as if that'll speed up the drying process.

I ask her about the stars,
    but am surprised by her nonchalant response.

          I dunno, she says,

          I'm kind of bored with astrology.

          I've been studying more of the Chinese zodiac.
          We're Year of the Horse, you know.

          Todd thinks it's pretty fascinating too.

She goes on
about the twenty-four solar terms
of the Chinese calendar—

    beautiful phrases that sound like poetry:

        limit of heat,

            frost descent,

               awakening of insects.

It's all interesting—but—
    as I listen,
        I get a skin-prickling
        humidity-like sickness.

          If Lola Sun is suddenly over star charts,
          then maybe things aren't done changing after all.

***

Right after Lola Sun leaves,
Mama receives a text from Garrett.

I'm okay, Heather Grace.

I'm okay.

School Reopens

Principal Keys makes the controversial call
to open schools up today.

> The next two counties over
> won't re-open until October,

>> but Keys stands firm in his decision.

Any more time off
cuts into teachers' summers,
and many work second jobs.

> Keys doesn't want half his staff
> to lose any more income.

Each morning we'll arrive
fifteen minutes early,
> depart fifteen minutes later
> in the afternoon.

It's not that much time
to cover the cost of what we lost in the hurricane,

> but at least it's extra homeroom time.

In the pale peach wash of morning sun—
> a sweet-tea-stained glaze of light—

> I reconfirm my journalist commitments,
> look over my vision board once more,

>> listen for Lola Sun's beep.

The Newspaper Staff Reconvenes, Assesses

Lola Sun and I are pretty much fine—
    our families and houses spared
    from serious damage.

Stephen's sloped front yard
    amassed so much rainwater,
    it's now practically a pond.

Todd's father's car caught a crashing pine.
    They think insurance will cover it,
    but they'll have to carpool with us for a while.

And Maya's sad that the group of feral cats
who hung out around her flat
    have disappeared.

      They probably drowned,
        but no one can bear
          to say that out loud.

Maria Renée fared the worst—

    half her roof torn off,
    her living room soaked,
      mold growing
      where the walls are exposed.

She barely speaks all period.

***

When Stephen sees my cracked phone screen,
he laughs.

> *Please tell me Florence winds forced it from your hand,*
> *that this poor machine isn't just a casualty of clumsiness.*

> I blush,
> snap back,

> *I can neither*
> *confirm nor deny—*

> *Hand it here, Millie,* he says.
> *I can fix it by morning.*

Todd Asks to Be Dropped Off after School

The purple dye in their hair a faded fuchsia,
    the weak pastel of stadium confetti,
    fallen and trampled on by fans.

The three of us walk to the parking lot,
    and Todd slips into the passenger seat—

    silently but sure,
    like how kudzu starts its slow, green creep
    over concrete and chain link.

Lola Sun blinks sheepishly back at me.

I buckle up in her messy back seat,
    a mass of plastic water bottles
    she means to recycle.

In this moment, I am demoted—

    our friendship downgraded
    on account of their romance.

Some Clouds Lose No Mass When It Rains

Their moisture continuously flows
thanks to a frontal system.

These clouds can pour
and still remain whole.

Others disappear depending on
if the flow is weakly sheared—

they lose their lower half,
top layers sublimating into vapor.

If I cry right now in this back seat,
it's over.

I'll become one of those clouds
that disintegrates into nothing
but memory and mist.

Surprise Visit

When I get home,
Garrett's voice sounds down the hall—
    shushed and secretive.

He and Mama must be discussing
something awful heavy.

    Their words hurried and hushed,
    dropping like crumbs on the kitchen counter.

I rush to hug him,
    his cedar wood cologne
    mixed with the sage of his aftershave.

He tries to joke around
the way we normally do,
but his voice is softer,
his forehead more furrowed.

    A permanent frown
    cast on his mouth.

He's safe,
but it's clear that,
    for him,
        the storm
            hasn't passed.

Off the Record

After about half an hour,
Mama asks me to

    go play in my room,

        like I'm a five-year-old child
        awaiting a babysitter.

Asks me to

    let the grown-ups talk,

        like that's not a huge red flag
        for an up-and-coming reporter.

Let the grown-ups talk
might mean one thing to Mama—

    permission to speak privately
    without eavesdropping ears—

    but what she says
    and what I don't hear
    are worlds apart.

        She said, *Let the grown-ups talk.*

        But I never heard,
            Off the record.

Fumes, It Started with the

gray fumes of smoke, says Garrett.

Faint at first.
Barely discernible as they twisted beneath
the kitchen's doorframe.

The scent floated to us next,
rose over the stench of unwashed pets.
Coated our throats. Everyone started to cough
as smoldering air lodged itself into our lungs.

Then, over the rain,
over the sinister whistle
of spinning wind,

we heard the blaze.

I Had to Get Everyone Out

That place was so poorly ventilated,
it was only a matter of moments
before the flames would take it.

Somehow, I was able
to shout loud enough
to herd humans and cats alike
into a single-file line.

People shivering, sobbing.
Clasping the last
of their belongings.

We marched to the pharmacy
across the street.

I opened it with the city key
and waited until Beatty sent help.

Among the rows of prescriptions and pills,
we watched the flames spill.

The crack and cackle
of wooden beams snapped in half
by the fire's frenzied teeth.

***

I'm so glad you got everyone out, baby,
Mama says. *I'm so glad you're safe.*

Do we know what started it?
Was it lightning that set off the flames?

Garrett shakes his head,
rubs the rough bristle of his jawline.
He stares at the floor,
but his eyes travel back in time.

    It was that damn volunteer, Heather Grace.
    The one who never listened.

       Eleanor Kearney is her name.

          She plugged an electric kettle
          into one of the bum outlets.

            Left it unattended and stepped outside,
            right in the middle of the wind and rain,

              to smoke a cigarette.

My Next Story

occurs to me as I tiptoe slowly
from the spot in the hallway
where I've been spying.

Back in my bedroom,
in front of my journalism board,
it starts to form.

It might not have a headline yet,
no shape or structure or plot,

    but it's got two things
    going for it—

        an anonymous eyewitness account

           and an unsuspecting subject:

                Eleanor Kearney.

Thursday, September 27th

Stephen Slides My Phone to Me,

the new screen smooth and crack-free,
protected by a layer of tempered glass.

I also increased your storage space, he says.

His eyes shift,
his grin lopsided—

he definitely did something shady
for these upgrades.

I hand him the money Ellis gave me,
but Stephen shakes his head.

Oh, please, Millie—that's peanuts,
pocket change compared to what I usually charge.

We laugh,
so distracted
we don't see Maria Renée leave.

It's only when we hear her voice
on The Morning Minute

we realize

she's about to drop

a surprise.

Maria Renée's Announcement

After she runs down
the school's post-storm policy changes—

> the end-of-semester's standardized testing dates
> pushed back two weeks,

>> the water fountains quarantined until further notice
>> since hog shit flooded into our riverways—

Maria Renée shares a message
that makes my head spin.

> *Finally*, she says, The Bloom *would like to make a special*
> *announcement.*

> *In the wake of Florence, it's even more important*
> *to offer thorough coverage of all our stories.*

>> *Therefore, we'll be expanding our masthead.*

> *Please join me in congratulating*

>> *Maya Nickleson*

>>> *as she becomes*
>>> *my new editorial assistant!*

***

Lightning strikes my spine,
    singes every nerve with a surge of anger.

When was this decided?

Lola Sun looks at me,
equally surprised.

    She scribbles down something quick,
    slips me a folded piece of paper.

      Dear Horse,

      We have just passed the Chinese autumn equinox—
          believe in balance.

      However much night you may be forced to hold within
          yourself,
          you'll be given the same amount of light.

      Soon comes Cold Dew.

      The world will seem chilled, but remember—
      it is not yet time for the first frost.

      There is still freedom here—
          move toward the southwest.
          Follow the scent of jasmine.

I can't even appreciate the kindness crafted in these words,
because I'm used to being a Capricorn,
                not some stupid horse.

And then I catch Todd's eyes—
        two blue rings wracked with real concern,

                but I need them
                        and their cheap pity

                        like I needed a storm surge
                        slamming into Mama's minivan.

***

When Maria Renée returns,
everyone makes a big show
of congratulating Maya.

> With the sparkle of gold glitter in her fro,
> it's as if she's walking beneath a spotlight
> secured just for her.

Maria Renée says,

> *Maya—more than anyone—*
> *searched for stories during the storm,*

> *and that's the kind of initiative I need.*
> *Here—look at this photo essay she sent me.*

Maya's Photos Are Stunning

Projected on our blackboard,
blown-up images of the wreckage.

I have no idea how she got so close to her subjects,
but each shot is framed with care.

Even as these peoples' expressions betray
devastation and heartbreak,

Maya's work never exploits them—
it simply documents the moment.

In one photo, a woman stands
on the front steps of a brick church,

blue water risen past the wheelchair ramp.

The church's steeple's been toppled sideways,
entangled in the wires of a fallen stoplight
somehow still lit.

A sign washed in bright red light,

the word *BAPTIST*

ablaze.

The Bloom's Unofficial Weather Report

Balmy, with a chance of betrayal.

Tonight's Live with Channel Five Report

is a litany of staggering hurricane statistics.

> Almost half a million evacuated,
> almost a dozen dams
> > breached
> > or
> > flooded.

> Over eleven-thousand homes with reported damage,
> the majority flood-related.

The city is still unsure, Felicia says,
to what extent weather
is to blame for the flames
that took down Lindley Library's west side.

The city, I think,
but not me.

> *Turn that woman off!*

> Mama hollers from one room over.

> *It's over now and everyone's safe.*
> *I've never heard a louder mosquito,*
> *buzzing in everyone else's business.*

Pesky insect or not,
Felicia only sacrifices subjects
if the blood is worth the story.

I snap the television off.

The Most Extensive Investigation

I've ever done as weatherwoman
is to literally walk out the front door.

What news can I share with my community
that they can't see for themselves through a window?

It's a powerless feeling,
to have ambition with no goals.
To not be entrusted with tasks,
a path of importance set before me.

But this lead
is what's gonna help me
succeed.

All night I search
for signs and stories,
clues and context.

Social media posts.
Old phone book listings.
Virtual family trees
and local land deeds.

Any sliver of backstory
to help explain
the subject of my exposé.

Who is Eleanor Kearney,
and what makes her the type of woman
to risk her life—and the lives of others—

to smoke a cigarette
in the face of Florence?

Emily Paige Wilson

Saturday, September 29th

Lola Sun Picks Me up for Coffee

We head to the local hipster café—
    brick walls and potted succulents
    hanging from beige macramé.

    It's been doing surprisingly well post-Florence,
    says the owner. *All these clean-up crews*
    need multiple cups of extra strong brew.

We sit at a table, sip iced chais
sprinkled with a powdered nutmeg blend.

And I present to Lola Sun
everything I've found out.

Eleanor Kearney: The Facts

Fifty-five years old.

Her only social media presence
is an infrequently used Facebook account.

> From her profile picture, it's hard to make out
> whether she dyes her gray hair pink
> or if her natural auburn faded with age.

> She stands outside, cigarette stub between her teeth,
> arms crossed over a black tank-top,
> the white lettering of some eighties band underneath.

Born in Magnolia, Eleanor Kearney
spent all her childhood days by the water.
Swimming, skiing, wake-skating.

The small house her parents rented
near the shore was destroyed
during Hugo.

> She studied biology at Berkeley,
> then seems to have come back
> to Magnolia, where she lives alone.

> The Google Street View of her house:
> maroon shutters and unwashed gutters,
> stray cats patting along
> an imperfectly planted row of purple pansies.

She's been part-time at Lindley Library
for the past five years—
   no prior employment history
   I could find online, but
   there is one misdemeanor on her record.

   Eleanor Kearney, in 1985,
   paid a thousand-dollar fine
   for a charge of indecent exposure.

Eleanor Kearney: The Evidence

I show Lola Sun screenshots
of all of Eleanor's Facebook hot takes.

Whelp, we haven't seen this much
CO_2 in the atmosphere
since trees grew at the South Pole
300 million years ago.

   Just wait until we hit that mark
   of 1.5 C°—that's when the real
   shitshow will start.

      How the hell do we live with ourselves
      when we've killed off
      60% of the world's wildlife?

The tone of each post
escalates in anger.

We did this to ourselves, she typed
back in 2016, the night before
Hurricane Matthew made it to shore.

   We did this to ourselves,
   and we deserve to die.

Lola Sun Stirs Her Chai,

stares through the window, and sighs.

Just because she posted that
doesn't mean she actually meant
to cause any harm at the shelter.

    Didn't Garrett himself say
    it was an accident?

Why isn't Lola Sun
as excited as I am?

I have everything I need
to craft the story of my career.

    I feel as if our friendship
    is collapsing into a black hole—
    mass and spin and a negative electric charge.

    We used to orbit each other perfectly,
    and now I'm sending out signals,
    hoping they'll be heard
    on the other side of the galaxy.

People's lives were at stake!
Magnolia deserves to know the truth.
This woman acted irresponsibly
and put dozens of citizens in danger.

She made a mistake.
She should be held accountable,
be made to pay.

Steam has stopped rising from our drinks,
the tea between us growing cold.

I know, I know, Lola Sun says,
and I don't disagree entirely.
But isn't it up to Garrett and the sheriff's office
to decide what to do with this information?

    No, I say, defiant
    as a dying hurricane.

        No, it's up to a reporter.

The Barista Sneaks Worried Glances Our Way

as we speak in an ever-increasing volume,
our voices washing over the small room.

I ran this scenario by Todd, Lola Sun says,
and they likened it to a three-point shot.

> *Yeah, it's great if an exposé pays off,*
> *but won't you feel foolish if it backfires,*
> *bounces off the rim?*

I press even further,
undeterred by her tepid attempts
to dissuade me from what could be
my professional destiny.

What if someone had pressured reporters
to run a story about how the city
refused to pay for proper signage
back when my daddy was still alive?

> *One story, one small story*
> *could have started a conversation,*
> *could have led to change.*
> *My dad could still be here today.*

Lola Sun Goes Too Far

Millie, this is not the same.
A story about road signs
could have saved lives, yes,

> *but this?*

> *Who would benefit*
> *if we blame this woman?*

> *Who is safer if we set a stage*
> *for the entire town of Magnolia*
> *to vent their rage over this one woman's mistake?*

She glides her hand
across the table to touch mine.

No story has the power
to bring back your dad,
you know that.

She whispers now,
the café grown crowded.

If you want me to be honest with you,
I don't think your main concern is safety.
I don't even think it's truth for truth's sake.

> *I think your main concern*
> *is the editorship at stake.*

Thank Goodness There Are No Cameras Rolling

because I lose it.

Messy and unprofessional.
Motivated by an anger so hot
Mama could sauté garlic in it.

> *You don't get to tell me*
> *what to think about my daddy*
> *and his death.*

Words seethe between my teeth,
tempered and mean.

> *Thanks for thinking that little of me*
> *that I would sell out some stranger for clout*
> *instead of wanting to do the right thing,*
>   *which is what this is really about.*

> *And I don't care—not now or ever—*
> *what Todd thinks.*

> *If I want a sports score—*
>   *a stupid basketball hot take,*
>   *superstar trade wars-type news,*

> *I'll ask them.*

> *But I'm trying to talk to* you
> *because—back before you had a partner—*

>   *we used to be best friends.*

All Lola Sun Says:

We used *to be best friends?*

Lola Sun Leaves

I don't cry as I wait for Mama to pick me up,

    not even as I drop my empty mug off at the counter
    and the barista smiles at me,

        a sad slope of a line that lets me know
        she overheard everything.

For the first time in weeks,
the sun is so bright
        I squint
        as I walk outside—
                a whitewash of light.

Mama arrives.
Her words simmer,
low and concerned.

    Is everything alright? I thought Lola Sun
    was gonna drop you back off.

I don't—I won't—tell her
about our fight.

She tries again.

    So, we heading home now, kiddo?

        No, I say, my voice watered-down, weak.

    I need to run an errand first.

I give Mama a street address
    and hope the owner will be home.

Mama Pulls up to a Hard-Hit House

Florence written in invisible cursive
across the crumbled roof.

> Blue tarp askew,
> a hole in clear view.

> > Large sheets of siding have been stripped,
> > burnt orange vinyl littered across the lawn's patchy grass.

The chaos theory of it all—

> so little but luck stood between
> which houses were hit

> > and which the storm
> > saw fit to spare.

I walk to the front door,
hear the soft dance of Spanish
move from mouth to ear.

I knock.
> Once,
> > twice.

> > *Hello?* I call.

> > *Maria Renée? Are you there?*

***

Maria Renée appears in a sweat-stained t-shirt,
denim shorts frayed mid-thigh.

    Her usual pageant posture swapped
    for slumped shoulders,
        arms crossed above her stomach.

She closes the front door quickly behind her.

    Millie, she says, *what are you doing here?*

I Pitch Her My Story

The insider scoop.

> Confirmation that the Lindley Library fire
> was not a result of inclement weather.
> The name of the human source of the flames.

I wait for her excitement,
> to ask me how I know.

> To retract Maya's position,
> > apologize for the rash decision,
> > offer it to me instead.

> > > But all I get is: *No.*

Maria Renée Elaborates

Do you know what these past few weeks
have been like for me, Millie?

Look at this house!

My parents don't know if insurance will pay out.
    If it doesn't,
                all they have saved is my college fund.

She starts to cry.

I can pretty much kiss my dreams goodbye.

My cousin's house is even worse.

    He's undocumented
    and can't get government aid.

First, we were worried about ICE raids,
    and now his house is a disaster.

        We can't catch a break.

I have an impulse to hug her,
but my arms stay limp by my side.

    My bruised shoulder surges and aches,
    the white-hot impact of empathy.

Maria Renée wipes tears from her face.

    Thanks for the idea, Millie, but no.

        With so much going on,
        I want The Bloom *to report on recovery,*
        not run a cheap defamation piece.

***

Back home, Mama makes vegan Brunswick stew for supper.

She's tried many plant-based substitutes before—
limp lentils and a tough block of tempeh—

but tonight, it's a new experiment:
hearts of palm to mimic the texture of shredded chicken.

Celery swelters in olive oil,
minced onions sweat.

Mama adds extra butter beans for me,
stirs in a can of sweet corn.

She ladles a large helping in two bowls,
needles her way back
into the controversy in the coffee shop.

Says, *Baby, whatever's going on,
don't be mad about it for too long—*

*it won't matter a hoot four months past now,
especially between best friends.*

With a heavy hand, she splashes hot sauce in my bowl,
and I let her think she's right.

***

As I rinse the copper pots clean,
my phone beeps—

here it is, Lola Sun's apology.

She'll admit our friendship's turned retrograde
        and how it's her fault
                for choosing Todd over me.

        How it's a shit accusation
        that all I care about is the editorship.

She'll admit—

        but, no—

                it's a message from Maria Renée.

                Hey. How sure are you
                that woman is the culprit?

Maria Renée Calls

I'm so pissed—after everything my family's been through,
now this.

A FEMA officer came by today,
and our family doesn't qualify for relief.

> *They suggested we take out a loan!*

> *A loan!*

The government wants to make money
out of our tragedy, so screw it—

> *if someone working for the state messed up,*
> *that's on them.*

> *They deserve to be exposed.*

***

As Maria Renée speaks,
I face my vision board.

It's not the journalists I look to now,
but the picture of Daddy,
        me on his knee,
          his smile wide and proud.

I need to know if I can actually do this
before we move forward.

What if Lola Sun is right?

What if I'm placing my own glory
over the integrity of this story?

Do I really think Eleanor Kearney
meant to set the library on fire?

    And does intention even matter
    when the aftermath is a literal fire,

        one that herded vulnerable citizens
        straight into the raging arms of a hurricane?

As long as everything I write
is based in truth,
        then can I stand confident
        in what I have to do?

***

Maria Renée hangs up, then sends one last text:

How soon can you get me the story?

IV. Two Weeks Past Florence

Emily Paige Wilson

Candied Yams with Maple and Pecans,

> *strawberry and cherry bruschetta,*
> *loafs of seitan savory as any roast!*

It's plenty appetizing! Mama hollers into the phone.

I motion toward the door,
    shrug the backpack straps
    on my shoulders dramatically.

Mama isn't used to this new routine
of taking me to school.

    Lola Sun and I still haven't spoken,
    and, anyway, Todd's taken my seat in her Beetle.

Mama nods but keeps coddling the phone.

> *No, I think it's a great idea!*
> *A post-Florence fundraiser at The Anchor!*

> *All I'm saying is,*
> *I want it vegan.*

> *The point is to raise money,*
> *not waste more resources on meat*
> *when I could cook vegan cheap!*

Pennies to the dollar
when we forgo prime ribs for collards.

Hmmmmm.

Mmmmhmmm.

> *Yes, I realize hog farmers are hurting right*
> *now,*
> *but—*

I sigh and silent-stomp my way to the car,
whisper, *We're gonna be late!*

Mama grabs the car keys,
keeps on blabbering sour as a crab apple
    to the poor soul on the phone,

> but at least it's the first time I've seen Heather Grace
> be Heather Grace
>   since Florence had her say.

***

We pull in right next to Lola Sun's punch buggy.
    Lola Sun and Todd sit in the front seats,
        and it almost feels like Mama's parked here on purpose.

Try to make peace today, kiddo, she says—

    this coming from the same woman
    who's gonna boycott a fundraiser
    over a little bacon fat.

I close the car door,
catch the dark cabochon
of Lola Sun's eye—

      and then Todd's,
      who somehow seems even sadder.

Homeroom's Never Loomed Heavy Before,

but now each step toward our office is a chore.

    I wear the weight of my exposé
    like an extra skeleton—

        what a relief it will be
        to shed this second set of bones.

Maria Renée pulls me over to her desk,
Stephen by her side.

      We've already formatted the file, she says.

        Say the word

          and we're live.

Breaking News from *The Bloom*

Shelter Staff Responsible for Lindley Library Fire
by Millie Willard, Staff Reporter

In the wake of Hurricane Florence, the Category Four storm responsible for 53 fatalities and billions of dollars in freshwater flooding damage, the people of Magnolia, SC, are left with numerous questions. How long until our main roads reopen, our waterways are free from debris, and our pipelines to gasoline and groceries accessible again? What we as a town should not be wondering, however, is if the state and its employees did their best to keep us safe.

While townspeople would hope the answer to that question would be a given, locals are left unsure after the events of Friday, September 21st. The 77 Magnolia residents and their pets who sought shelter in Lindley Library were forced into an immediate evacuation after the library's west side caught on fire. Speculation has swirled over whether the blaze was a result of a lightning strike or an electrical fire caused by the record-breaking levels of rain.

Thanks to an anonymous source, *The Bloom* is the first to report the fire originated in the library's small kitchen when 55-year-old part-time librarian and shelter staff member Eleanor Kearney plugged an electric kettle into an ungrounded outlet and then abandoned her post to take a smoke break outside.

The building's aging infrastructure, poor ventilation, and a row of inoperable windows accelerated the rate at which the fire spread. Local law enforcement officers stationed at the shelter were able to relocate everyone inside to the nearby pharmacy, preventing any injuries or deaths. The total cost of personal belongings lost in the fire has yet to be calculated. While the fire seems to have been an accident, Sheriff Beatty's office has yet to make any public comment on whether it plans to charge Ms. Kearney and to what extent.

This story is still developing. For further updates, be sure to check back frequently with *The Bloom*.

On Site

Maya gets Principal Keys's permission
for us to shoot photographs on site—

> a field trip to the charred library,
> the building's rusted, exposed skeleton
> covered in slate-colored dust.

Maria Renée drives Maya and me,
    takes the long way through town
      to avoid all the water-wound roads,
        the closures chaos caused.

Yellow tape is strung along the structure,
draped and dangled between the branches
of the battered palms that line the entrance's sides.

> A hurried spider's web,
> messy circles of caution
> haphazardly hung.

We sit in silence as Maya adjusts her lens,
    focuses on the infrastructure that failed
    against the angry flames.

Maya's shutter clicks, snaps.

Alright, she says,
slinging the camera strap across her shoulder.
I think we have what we need.

The Rest of the Day Is a Waiting Game

Like time is a piece to play,
but my turn is perpetually skipped,
      round after round.
         Hand after hurricane hand.

I wait during second period—
      not a whisper of my report,
      just the scratch of chalk on blackboard,

      but I'm too distracted for fractals
      or notes on nuclear fission.

Nothing at lunch—
      no one shouting the news over the crunch of celery,
      the cracking open of soda cans.

During final period, Mr. Daldry's voice drones on
until some poor soul raises his hand,
asks, *But I don't understand?*

      The room groans, bemoans the fate
      of this poor soul who didn't know better
      than to fake comprehension.

I'm sorry, Daldry says,
his familiar response put on
with theatrical flair,
but was there a question in there?

If you don't ask me the right questions,
how can I help you find the right answers?

I check on the article again
as we're assigned a hefty hunk of homework—
    not so much as a single comment.

I head home, nothing left to lose
except my patience.

    Did I take an enormous professional risk
    just to have the story slip
    into online oblivion?

And Then It Begins

The same way hurricanes form—
movement so slow the storm
doesn't realize it's taking shape
          until it's too late.

A rise in temperature—
    so subtle as to not even register on the skin.

      A westward wind.

        A cluster of cumulonimbus clouds—
        their coverage the first shadowy sign.

A draft.

    A disturbance.

      A depression
      that threatens thunderstorms.

My story's spread begins
with one ping—

      each beep, a retweet—

        the link favorited, forwarded.

          Every share streamed on my phone screen.

          The storm doesn't even realize
          it's taking

            shape.

The Bloom Is Bombarded

with telephone calls and emails,
reporters as far away as Charleston
asking to pick up the story,

> questioning our code of ethics,
> and ensuring our editor
> can verify the identity
> of our anonymous source.

The inundation's even worse
on social media.

There's so much online traffic,
it almost crashes our site.

> Every Magnolia resident
> hell-bent on publishing their opinions
> for others to read.

> The good, the bad,
> and the downright mean
> circulating across my computer screen.

> A twinge of pity hits me,
> and I'm glad Eleanor isn't active enough online
> to see how often she's tagged,
> her name dragged through the social media mud.

But all of this is bigger than one person.
The city now knows the truth,
and I started this conversation with my story.

Me, a junior weatherwoman
who used to be relegated to just the rain.

One Tweet Takes Them All to Task

One account—certified blue checkmark—
    retweets the article's link,

        hypes *The Bloom* as a bona fide news source,
        congratulates my colleagues

            for their professionalism
            at such a young age,

                but then name-checks me specifically.

                    Spotlight on high school junior Millie Willard.

                    Star reporting from a promising new voice!

My heart quickens,
    the slick patter of fox paws
    slinking near a chicken coop.

It's Felicia Fitz!
    I really am
    about to be famous!

Felicia's Tweets Take a Turn for the Worse

Proud to see young people
holding the state accountable.

> *Now we just have to get answers*
> *from Eleanor Kearney herself.*

> > *#SheltersShouldBeSafe*
> > *#CallOutKearney*

Everyone's Reaction

Maria Renée: *I'm proud of you, Millie. Maybe we should consider a co-editorship next year with you and Maya?*

Maya: *What a good team we make, Millie!*

Stephen: *Damn it—I would've reformatted the dimensions for better desktop compatibility if I'd have known this thing would blow up.*

Todd:—Their eyes bob back and forth between me and Lola Sun. They lob looks like a ball across some sports court and then thumbs-up me under their desk. A small, unexpected sign of kindness.

Lola Sun: Silence.

Mama's Too Busy

mapping out a menu
to notice the morning news—

> Channel Five's flashing banner,
> *#CallOutKearney*—

>> but I know it's a matter of time
>> before she finds out about the exposé.

>> How I broke a story to the world
>> based on what Garrett told her
>> in confidence.

My handle streams across the screen,
my social media followers up a full hundred flush
since my first cup of coffee.

Almond creamer spools
into my dark pool of caffeine—

> swirls in slow spirals
> like the guilt in my conscience.

Mama! I holler.
Homeroom's in fifteen! Let's go!

> It's a strange sensation,

>> this pride in my reporting
>> infused with the fear
>> of Mama finding out.

What Mr. Daldry Says

My, my, Millie, he chides,
straightening his tie,
cross-stitched with red pie charts.

> *All that time you spent*
> *scribbling in the back of class—*

> > *I knew you looked too excited*
> > *to be taking notes on graphs.*

What Principal Keys Says

Well, Miss Willard, I am pleasantly surprised.

> *You finally figured out*
> *how to match your tenacity with your talent.*

> *We need more of that in the future—*
> *first-rate reporting.*

> *No more mayhem in the margins,*
> *no more makeshift Morning Minutes.*

We smile, neither one of us acknowledging how
    I've never not been called into his office before
    unless it was on account of trouble.

> How quickly the tides turn,
> churn toward fame and fortune.

> Toward a stern principal's good favor.

Hidden in My Locker

is a folded piece of paper,
shoved through the slot—

      my first ever fan mail!

I'll save it, frame it,
      maybe tape it to my vision board.

The writing on the note is haggard,
haphazard letters scribbled
so closely together they look choked.

      I've seen this chicken scratch scrawl
      somewhere before.

          Oh, my god—this handwriting
          is Todd's.

Todd's Note

Hey, Millie,

> *I'm not as strong with words as Lola Sun.*

> *This note isn't spun with star-shine*
> *and it can't predict the future—*

> *but Lola Sun misses you.*

>> *And she's proud but can't admit it—*
>> *we're all proud of your story!*

Apparently, an Aquarius becomes detached when upset—
floats off on the hot air of their hurt feelings.

Let me put it to ya in sports terms.

> *You're having your quarterback moment—*

>> *the rush of yards—*

>>> *the touchdown!*

But Lola Sun's still your best edge pass-rusher.

She will go to great lengths to shorten the field for you.

What People Say During Lunch

There's so much commotion
I almost don't notice
    Lola Sun and Todd
three tables away from me.

I sit next to Maya and Maria Renée,
but I can barely get a bite in.

    Maria Renée asks for my next feature idea.

    I know it's quick turnaround, she says,
    but this is what editor life is like.
    Gotta draft your next story while the last one's still hot.

I'm saved from an on-the-spot pitch
as students from all social cliques swarm us.

    The theater kids—including the spray-paint detention bandit
    —all want headshots by Maya,
        reviews written by me of their *King Lear* production
        premiering next month.

    The science nerds need to take out ad space
    to showcase their new remote-controlled robot.
        They offer enough money to fund two complete issues of *The Bloom*.

But by far, the most surreal request comes from the cheer captain.

She would've never spoken to me two days ago,
but here she is networking like it's nothing.

So, Millie, I need a profile piece written on me,
but we need to move quickly.

I want, like, a senior portrait, but in words.
Does that sound cool?

But, like, not quite like your Kearney report—
   I need you to make me look good.

My Phone Pings So Often,

I turn it off—
it's practically hot at this point.

    Each app's icon looks like
    it will topple
        under the weight
    of the inflated red notification balloons.

Snapchat, Twitter, even my email!
The thrill of each shrill ping—
    unsure whether it's praise or outrage.

    The dopamine rush,
    the crutch of scrolling.

Geez, Maria Renée says and lifts the lunch trays
we've barely picked over, takes them to the trash.

    Millie, this is even more media attention
    than when I lost Miss Magnolia.

What Going Viral Feels Like

It doesn't take much to convince Mama
not to turn on the news tonight.

> She says she's had enough
> slick lip service from Felicia Fitz
> for one hurricane season.

We spend a quiet evening at home,
even though I'm a hit on the internet.

Going viral is wild.

> It feels like it should change everything,
> yet most of my life has remained the same.

> It feels like being the smartest person
> in an empty room.

> It feels like a twister sickness
in my stomach—

> sometime soon
> one of these responses
will belong to Garrett.

> Sometime soon,
> I'll discover if the blowback
> is worth being a reporter.

And while I stand by my version of the truth,
why do I feel this swamp sludge of ruthlessness?

As the social media mob begins its pile on of Eleanor—
    signs posted in yards around town,
    taped to convenient store windows
    calling her *Kearney the Hurricane Killer*—

        why am I starting to feel more like a fake
        and less like a hero?

        What if Lola Sun was right,
        and I'm spreading not so much as facts
        but a brutal wave of backlash?

I Tell Mama a Lie

I tell her Lola Sun and I made up,
that she'll take me to school today.

That Mama can head straight to The Anchor this morning
and won't have to worry about drop-offs and pick-ups.

Sounds good, baby! I'm glad.
Y'all run together thick as weeds, she says.

A pink streak of shame flames my cheeks,
but I wave her off to work.

Lola Sun and I haven't spoken in days,
not since the coffee shop fiasco—
when I told her we *used* to be friends.

I didn't know it then,
but turns out it was the truth.

Lola Sun's not picking me up,
and I'm not going to school.

What with all the social media comments
to which I've yet to respond,

the responsibility of drafting up my next big story,

I deserve one damn day to play hooky.

What a Magnolia October Should Be Like

Golden and crackling as caramel slow cooked on the stove.

The spiced scent of cinnamon.

The wind whispering for sweaters,
each tree a web of orange leaves.

October should smell of oak moss and amber,
sound like the clamor of costumed kids.

But as I walk to the park
to spend my skip day,

the world feels no nearer
to county fair season
than it did in January.

The air still smells like the hog shit
that washed into the rivers,

the trees' bare black branches,

scarecrows of their former selves.

And the humidity's hanging around
like apples reluctant to drop and rot—

no crisp, cool air here.

Even when she's gone,

Florence still dictates the weather.

Out of the Blue

As I sit on a park swing, swish forward and back,
my feet graze what's left of the grass.

A Morse code of mosquito bites
reddens my bare skin,
    but I don't mind the itch—

    it's better than sentence fragments
    and split infinitives any day.

I check my newsfeeds,
the tweets and streams of snaps.

    I scroll mindless,
    making sure they're mostly positive—
        endorsements for my journalism work.

    And then the barrage of hateful comments
    targeted at Eleanor—a hashtag parade
    of *#CallOutKearney*.

Someone asks, *How did the fire fuck over your family?*
and response after response explains the pain
of those who had loved ones inside Lindley—

My younger brother was in there!
He could have burned to death!

My mother's asthma attacks
have gotten ten times worse!

A call to charge Eleanor with reckless endangerment
takes center stage among all the outrage.

I look up, away from the contagion of anger.

Mid-morning sunlight glazes
the park's pond, a plate of molten gold.

Silence except for a chorus of cricket chirps,
    a few frogs croaking.

    And then my phone rings—
    an unknown number
    lighting up the screen.

***

Normally, I'd ignore an unknown number,
    but now that I'm technically small town famous,
    it seems irresponsible to do.

What if it's a secret tip-off for my next story?

    What if it's BuzzFeed asking for an exclusive feature?

       How would Felicia Fitz
       approach these opportunities?

         Always on the hunt
         for an unknown scoop—

         a hunch, a hint,
         some juicy admission.

To live life with this excited suspicion
that the next story's just one unexpected turn away.

I rehearse my response to this unknown caller
quickly in my mind,
       so quickly I slip,
       misspeak into the receiver—

       You've reached Felicia Fitz.
       I'm ready for whatever details you have to dish!

***

A laugh—plastic and polished—
glosses over the line.

Ummmm, I think you're mistaken, ma'am.

I'm Felicia Fitz,
and I'm calling for a Miss Millie Willard.

***

A few things going forward, sweetie,
Felicia continues.

> I haven't exhaled at all since she started speaking,
> afraid to breathe static into the receiver,

>> as if that crackling sound
>> will break the spell she's cast

>> because no way is this real.

Be sure to tag me and Channel Five
every time you repost your story from here on out.

And use the hashtag #CallOutKearney.
We want all our branding to be consistent,
and it's already trending.

And don't—under any circumstances—
respond to other media outlets
should they reach out—

>> *gotta keep our exclusive, well—exclusive.*

I swear I hear her wink.

> *Oh, Millie,* she says,

>> *we're gonna make a great team.*

***

I rush home—
    run through weeds and brambles.
    Mosquito bites seep on my thighs.

    I don't even care about the hog shit air anymore—

        I pump my legs, breathe in deep.

        As if I must move swiftly enough
        not to let this moment slip away.

Who would have thought it'd be Florence
to push my career forward,
    furious storm that ate our coast in a frenzy.

I jerk the front door open as I reach home—

    flushed and sweaty—

    and come face to face

        with Mama and Garrett.

Mama Goes Off

Her voice slides further and further
up the Scoville scale as she yells—

    bell pepper at first,
    barely worth the mention,

    to hot-tempered habanero
    to deadly dragon's breath.

In ten seconds flat,
    she's full-on hollering at me
    with all the heat of a Carolina Reaper.

What the hell were you thinking, Millie?

    It's all over the news!

        My sous chef—my sous chef!—said,
        'Hey, is that your Millie's name on TV?'

        And I had to stand there
        practically punch-drunk, dumbfounded.

          You leaked what Garrett said to me in secret?

          For what? For some byline to go viral?
          For a shot at some measly, sleazy five o'clock time slot?

            Just what exactly is it
            you hoped to accomplish?

***

I want to protest,
to tell Mama that the truth
is its own accomplishment,

    but Garrett speaks first.

Soft as a river's ridge,
    dirt that's slowly eroding
    but knows better than to argue
        with the water's rage.

        Millie, I've always loved that impatient streak in you,
        the impulse to push forward what you believe,
        but this whole thing reeks of disaster.

           Do you know why I hadn't reported
           the incident to Beatty?

               Two big reasons, kiddo,
               both of which you've blown past.

Garrett's First Reason

The state was so short-staffed
that we had to recruit people
with part-time employment.

Do you think I liked relying on their labor?

The state don't pay 'em health benefits
but demands they risk life and limb

and would send 'em swimming downstream
just as soon as the weather turns mean.

Eleanor was a pain in my ass,
but she made a mistake.

How was her leaving the kettle on
any different than when Mrs. Marguerite
'bout burned her whole street down?

Eleanor stayed and paid her dues
more so than any citizen that fled,
and now the town's threatening lawsuits.

Garrett's Second Reason

Now that there's such a commotion—
Magnolia panicked into a manic anger—
we have to use resources we ain't got
to make sure Eleanor stays safe.

We have a patrol person stationed
outside her house all day and night
to protect from incoming threats to her person.

Do you know where those officers should be?
Cleaning debris off the roads,
delivering food and supplies to distribution centers.

For every hour stationed at Eleanor's house,
that's an hour the people of Magnolia are not being helped out.

Garrett Finishes His Fatherly Speech

on the most punishing note possible.

> *To leak a secret—that's not how reporting works.*

> *I know you wanted to do what was right,*
> *I know you didn't mean to hurt nothing—*

>> *but so far, you've only succeeded*
>> *in making things worse.*

Emily Paige Wilson

The Ride to School Is Hot as a Crock Pot

Tension flints off Mama's skin in sparks
like fatback, all crackle and snap.

I swear to god, Millie—her voice a vinegar hiss.

Just go to school and behave. For one day.

And so help me, if I hear of one hiccup,
one false slip,
> *I'll pull you outta that journalism class*
> *faster than you can switch a news channel.*

Small Storms Are Called Thundershowers

Same wind, but weaker,

    not powerful enough to sustain thunder, but still,
        a temper tantrum in the sky.

Once at school, I stomp down the halls,
slam my locker—

    my bad energy more static electricity than lightning,
    but charged nonetheless and looking to strike.

It falls on Maria Renée
to be the grounding rod
for my jolt of anger.

    Right as homeroom bell rings,
    she says to me,
        Hey, Millie, forget the second feature for now—
        this week's weather report is overdue.

***

Excuse me? I say.
　　My words storm,
　　　　swirl around the room.

Maria Renée cuts her eyes at me—
　　narrows like the leaves
　　　　that fold their edges in
　　　　　　to protect themselves from tempests.

I said, she says,
　　clears her throat,
　　　　projects as if on a pageant stage.

　　　　The weather report is due.
　　　　Past due, actually.

　　　　　　I need it by the end of homeroom,
　　　　　　so I'd get to it if I were you.

She's too much of a professional
　　to be tempted into a petty contest,
　　　　but I won't give her any other choice.

No, I say, *I won't do it.*

***

The room stirs around us—
    a chair scratches the floor,
    a cough faked,
    faint and worried whispers.

I storm on:

    You're just jealous
    we're over your fifteen minutes of fame,
    and now it's my turn.

    I'm done being weatherwoman.
    It's a shit gig, a filler spot.

    I'm bigger than that now—
    I put The Bloom *on the map.*

    All of Magnolia's talking about my story!

        From now on, assign me real news—
                or I'm out!

***

No, Millie, Maria Renée says quietly.

Why is it always this?

These whispers of a threat
from Garrett and now her

that sound so much louder
than any shouting.

This is not what the fury of Florence taught me.

If you want to behave like this,
then I'm *out.*

She grabs her backpack and walks out the door.

***

Someone sitting at a desk behind me snickers—
    a mean sort of snort,
    a sound of severe disappointment.

Lola Sun stands up and steps close to me.

    Our hearts two white dwarf stars
    rotating around each other,
        dangerously close to collision.

What the hell, Millie? she spits.

She slides her heart-shaped frames past her nose,
the better to cast a belittling glance at me.

    Why are you being such an asshole?

Lola Sun glows in her anger—
    celestial sweat on her forehead,
    black hole eyes collapsed.

      She spends so much time reading the stars
      that I imagine them as sure and steady,

      but I forget they, too, implode.

Lola Sun Attacks

I didn't know an Aquarius
could get mad like this,

    but there are asteroids in her speech—
    a supernova at her feet.

        All you care about right now is yourself, Millie!

        Have you thought about how the storm's affected
        anyone else?

          No, you haven't!

        All Florence has meant to you is your stupid story—
        a chance to kiss ass for the editorship.

        Who have you helped? Who?
        No one. Not us, not Garrett,
        not those citizens in the shelter.

        You think it's so hard being weatherwoman—
        that it's so beneath you to write about clouds?

        How's this for a wakeup call?

        Todd gets threats every time they publish a sports piece—
          a few football players call them the f-word,
          say sports is no place for "queers," use that word like a slur.

Poor Maya—geometry's got her so tangled up
    in acute and obtuse angles,

I've been tutoring her twice a week,
    but you wouldn't know that, would you?

And Maria Renée—bless her—
    she's gonna lose it all, Millie.

The college scholarships she fought so hard for—
    her family still has to repair their roof.

We've all got battles to fight
    and here you are—

creating your own so you can be a hero.

And Then She Strikes Low on Purpose

It's a sad sack of shit excuse to pretend
you wrote this story for public safety—

> *this is just a Millie Willard*
> *personal publicity campaign.*

> *This is not what your dad would have wanted.*
> *You haven't made him proud.*
> *You haven't helped anyone in his name,*
> *and that's the real shame.*

At Home, It's a Battle of Stoniness

Both Mama and me embittered to the bone.

She's mapping out a menu again—
    the kitchen counter cluttered
    with recipe cards she keeps rearranging.

Finally, I break—
    can't take one more friend or family member
        being mad at me.

So, I ask, *is this for the charity event?*

She *hmmps* in acknowledgment,
    so I needle her further.

        Any exciting new appetizers?
        Trying your hand at different desserts?

Her eyes fix on my face,
turn into a food scale.

    She weighs the cost of opening back up—

        her anger in ounces,
        forgiveness in fluid milliliters,

        which hangs heavier?

She sighs.

Yes, Millie.

Here—I'll show you what I've cooked up.

It's gonna be Halloween-themed, she says,
shows me her recipe card spread.

An electric yellow-orange soup
stewed from carrots and ginger—

cilantro leaves sprinkled on top for garnish.

I want each bowl to look like a pumpkin.

Orange bell peppers carved into jack-o-lanterns,
guacamole-stuffed.

Pumpkin pies cooked with coconut cream.

*I figured it was a fitting theme
since the fundraiser's on the twenty-ninth.*

*It'll probably be an all-day event,
prep starting the night before—*

The twenty-ninth? I say without thinking.
*That's two weeks after my interview.
This is gonna be a busy month for us!*

Mama's face solidifies back to stone.

What interview?

Why Do I Even Tell Mama Anything Anymore?

Millie Willard, she says,
don't you dare speak to that woman!

> *Every time—every—single—time—*
> > *I think we've reached boiling point—*
> > *the steam upsetting the pot's top—*
> > *you raise the stakes.*

> *I don't know what to say to you anymore.*

Monday, October 8th

The Bloom's Official Weather Report

Light rain. Broken cloud coverage.

Here's the Thing about Meteorology

Weaving weather measurements
together into a story—

    it's not really meant for day-to-day forecasts.

Most meteorologists focus
on long-term shifts in weather systems—

    any specifics about a given day
    are little more than speculations.

      The same is true for relationships—

        the changes from day to day
        prove hard to predict.

          And though a few thousand
          social media followers
            after my article's launch
            made me feel real slick and accomplished,

            turns out they aren't as fulfilling
            as having real friends around.

I wake early,
walk the three blocks
to the nearest bus stop.

    I don't wanna rely on Mama or Lola Sun
    or anyone else for a ride,

        not when the tide of everyone's temper
        is set against me.

The bus takes a route I'm unused to—
    through the city's south side,
    where the storm's debris is still being cleaned.

Slumped shoulders of sidewalks
are cautioned off with orange tape
waving in the wind—
    crumpled concrete that buckled.

The frames of mold-ruined mattresses,
rain-soaked couches left outside for county pick-ups.

    Over five-thousand South Carolina families
    in need of FEMA assistance.

        Florence officially listed as an "incident"
        whose impact lasted from September 8th until today—

        an entire month's worth of monstrosity—

        but it's not as if our fight is over.

No one's in homeroom
    besides Stephen and Todd,

        worry warping both their faces
        past the point of words.

Should I even ask? I say anyway,
already anticipating what Stephen has to say.

        You screwed up, Millie.

        Lola Sun and Maya—they're not gonna show.

        Maria Renée said she doesn't care
        if the newspaper goes to hell,

        says she can afford one bad grade
        even if she fails this class.

            She said if you want this responsibility so badly,
            you can have it.

Stephen breathes out hurriedly,
    relieved he successfully
    memorized and relayed
    Maria Renée's speech to me.

Speaking for himself, he says,

        That was a lot of bridges to burn, Millie,
        but Todd and I,

            we're still here to help.

Even with Their Help,

unexpected difficulties arise.

Millie, you're not bleeding the margins right.

Millie, what's the budget code for printing again?

4692?
4691?

Millie, where's the receipt for the drama class's two-page ad?

King Lear?

Hamlet?

Was it even Shakespeare?

Even Todd pesters me with their questions.

Millie, do you think two back-to-back
soccer player profiles would be too much?

Huh, Millie?

Huh?

I splash cold water on my face
in the bathroom,
       as if the shock
       could erase the incompetence
       and confusion clogged in my pores.

My skin flushed,
     my hair a frenetic halo of frizz.

I don't see an editor in the reflection,
     not even a reporter—

          just a girl who didn't know
          the ins and outs

          of what she was talking about.

I Eat Lunch Alone in the Restroom

Try to balance the flimsy Styrofoam tray on my knees,
    but something about Sharpie-scrawled
    phone numbers on dirty tiles
    makes meatless fish sticks even less appealing.

On my way to third period,
I catch sight of Lola Sun and Todd
    holding hands in the hallway—happy—
                stars or no stars.

Her tie-dye skirt
the same shifting soft waves of blue
    that have been feathered into Todd's hair—

      and, damn,

        they are cute
        together.

Tears fill my eyes as I realize
how stupid my jealousy is.

        I walk in their direction,
        think maybe I'll apologize
        and then my phone beeps.

        Millie, call me
        if you haven't already heard the news.

      —FF

On the phone, Felicia
has a lilt in her voice,
    a lift
      from being listened to
         so attentively.

It doesn't seem like anyone was hurt,
but an attack was made on Eleanor Kearney.

    Well, her property—
      not her person, to be exact.

Apparently, she went to the library
to collect a leave of absence check
      and found her tires slashed.

Death threats taped to her door,
written on library fine receipts.

    You couldn't write a story sequel with more poetic justice—
      couldn't pen a punchline with more panache.

Felicia, why are you telling me this? I ask.

Before, this opportunity would've seemed
like the perfect open door,
                              but now
I'm skeptical,
            hesitant
            as a poorly
                    skipped
                          stone.
Yeah, it's a chance for another big byline,
but who's it doing right by?

Felicia's voice lowers,
her tone less friendly.

Why, Millie—I thought you'd be excited.
I'm handing you a lead
because I want to see you succeed.

I'll hold off on reporting this story
if you want to run it in The Bloom *first.*

Our viewership will respond well to one reporter—
especially a new, stand-out student voice—
following through with the same story.

You just have to write it quickly.

My Response

I'm sorry, Felicia,
but I have serious reservations.

Who would benefit from reporting
on Eleanor's death threats?

It doesn't make anyone safer or smarter.
It's just fodder for drama.

    Millie, Millie, Millie, she tsks.

    Disappointment
          drips
             in short syllables.

    The bell rings for my next class.

It's sweet that you're still at the stage
when morals matter, but

a reporter who doesn't care about ratings
isn't going to make it far.

I want to report the news, I say, *the truth.*
Not fan local gossip's fizzled out fire.

Felicia sighs as I scurry down the hall,
scrunch the phone between
my shoulder and cheek.

Let's get one thing clear, she says,
or you have no chance of a career.

Reporters must maintain a delicate balance.

And I don't mean to berate you, darling,
but you want to make a change?

First you have to prove
that you can bring in the ratings.

Tuesday, October 9th

Stephen Offers to Drop Me Off

after school again,
then asks me why my nerves are shot.

I can't get over it—death threats.
It doesn't make any sense.

> *People are mad Eleanor could have killed someone,*
> *so the solution is to threaten to kill her instead?*

Stephen sighs.

> *Millie, what did you think was going to happen?*

> *The town thinks she could've burned the whole library down.*
> *There were almost one hundred people in there.*
> *And don't forget the dozens of pets!*

I stretch the seat belt from my neck.

Felicia once said—

> before she tried to pressure me
> into some second-rate clickbait story—

that when your words are a wreck,
you need to start again at the source.

We have to go back to the library, I say.
Maybe even see if we can get inside.

> *No way!* Stephen says.
> *Wouldn't that be breaking and entering?*
> *Tampering with a crime scene?*

Stephen, I say,
it's for a story.

245

Lindley Library looks similar to when I saw it last week—

>how far into the past it feels
>since Maya and Maria Renée and I
>took pictures on a free period—

but different too,

>as if the days of public exposure
>have aged the burned building further.

>>The remaining windows cast
>>in a more saturated yellow,
>>as if the glass knows there's nothing left
>>worth looking through to.

Stephen convinces me not to sneak inside,
but we take photos on my restored phone.

Could you imagine how stupid and scared
Eleanor must have felt? Stephen asks.

You sneak out for one dumb cigarette
and return to a wave of smoke,
a wall of outraged faces.

He sighs as we sit down
on the library's front lawn.

A patch of scorched grass
within hand's reach of our feet.

Stephen continues.

I know everyone was obsessed
with figuring out how the fire started,

but what if that wasn't the right question?

What if we should've been asking
how this whole mess
could have been prevented?

The Right Questions

What did you say?

Stephen repeats himself.

I said, we figured out how—

> *No! No! About the right question.*

> I'm struck with such an abrupt suddenness
> that my vision swims, my head hums
> with the force of hurricane winds.

> *Damn it, maybe Daldry's been right this whole time.*
> *To get the right answers, we have to ask the right questions.*

Stephen squints.

What do you mean?

I pull browned and broken
stalks of grass from the earth,
dig my fingers into the dirt.

> *It's like what you said:*

> *How could this whole mess have been prevented?*
> *Why was a part-time librarian—*

> *untrained and underpaid—*

> *called upon to act like a member*
> *of the National Guard?*

Garrett's said it again and again—
everyone is underfunded.

No extra emergency money,
not enough shelters in town.

It's not like hurricane season is a surprise,
and ocean levels and coastal temperatures
continue to rise.

Why was our community so underserved,
and how can we get it the resources it deserves?

You're brilliant, Stephen! I say,
a tentative idea for my next feature
forming in my head.

Now you'll have to let me pay you back
for this brainstorming session.

Millie, he says,
waving his hand before my face.
It's for a story.

I Review My Vision Board at Night

My altar of journalists
who've made tougher decisions than mine,

    fixed worse mistakes
    before a much larger audience.

        Journalists accused of burying the lede,
        selling their networks short to succeed.

Others have lost their jobs, have faced far more
public shame to share the truth,

    and here I've been feeling sorry for myself,
    hiding alone in my room.

    But my story did cost me.

        My friends won't speak to me—

        Mama can't stand the sight of me—

        a stranger's getting death threats—

            and this newspaper has to get published
            even though I can't make heads or tails

                of the complicated mess of steps
                necessary to get it to print.

Every respectable journalist issues corrections
when they realize they've printed a mistake.

> And I still stand by the truth of my exposé,
> but now I realize the problem's larger context,
> how much more there is to say.

It might not be a full-fledged plan,
but it's a path for how to make things better
before they could possibly get any worse.

When I Come Home from School,

The kitchen counter is a laboratory
of cold cuts—slabs of pink meat
with slick swirls of marbled fat.

    Ham hocks and shredded chicken.
    Beef tips to be braised,
    marinating in a glaze of ginger and soy.

Even more surprisingly, Channel Five
is streaming on the TV—

    Felicia interviewing a local attorney
    on the steps of the courthouse
    about the viability of a potential
    reckless endangerment suit.

Mama? I say,
    tentatively approaching the kitchen
    as my vegan mother
    maniacally swings a butcher's knife—

      a whack,
      the crack of knotted pig knuckles.

Mama, what is all this?

Plum-colored blood stains her apron.
    She wipes forehead sweat
    with the back of her hand.

Wash up, Millie, she commands.

    Garrett's coming over for supper,
    and I reckon he has something important to tell ya.

***

Normally, the savory scent of meat
is a welcome and unexpected treat—

    the warm roasting of bacon in grease,
    crispy fried chicken skin.

But it's all I can do now
as I get ready for supper
not to get sick to my stomach—

      the heavy perfume of pulled pork
      permeates through my shower's steam,
      the uneasy green needles of nausea
         prickle through my cheeks.

Garrett Arrives

He sees the meat-heavy spread set before him
and manages a muddled laugh.

Heather Grace, he says,

> *It's not like I have an aversion to vegetables.*
> *I ain't allergic to greens.*

***

Mama chides Garrett for being too thin,
scoops two helpings' worth
of mashed potatoes on his plate.

With his hands folded on the small swell of his stomach,
he begins:

> *Now, Millie, I've already told this to Heather Grace,*
> *but I thought I'd tell you in person too.*
>
> *For her protection, Beatty has ordered Eleanor*
> *to stay in Charleston until things die down,*
> *and he's assigned me to be stationed with her.*
>
> *I'll be damned if I wouldn't rather stick around—*
> *can't help Magnolia rebound two hours away—*
> *but I ain't about to argue with what Beatty has to say.*

My brain swirls
like a broken weathervane.

> *Slashed tires is one thing,*
> *but it can get worse.*
>
> *Easily. Quickly.*
>
> *It's not permanent—*

his laugh is mirthless now,
a murky slurp of sound—

> *but hurricane season ain't even over.*
> *Who knows how much more trouble*
> *the weather's set in store for this town?*

***

Garrett, I say, *you should stay!*
I have an idea that will help
heal things over.

    It's just a rough draft,
    an outline really, but—

Millie, he says,
I love you,
but right now
the last thing I need
is another one of your stories.

***

When Garrett leaves,
Mama cleans the kitchen.

> I don't even bother to offer help
> because she'll turn down my company.

> This whole dinner a stage show to let me know
> she thinks the blame for Garrett leaving rests on me.

I text Lola Sun:

> *Hey—it's me—please.*
> *I need your help.*

Five minutes later:

> *Please?*

An hour:

> *It's about our next feature.*
> *I think I've figured it out.*
> *How we can maximize*
> *this current publicity*
> *and actually be of more help.*

Then I call—it rings repeatedly.

I call once more—
      straight to voicemail.

> I've agitated Lola Sun so much
> she straight up turned her phone off.

I Know I Shouldn't Check My Phone

during math class,
but my attention is spiraling

more sloppily than the slope on this graph.

    Ever since Garrett's left,
    it's easier to scroll on social,

        indulge in the brightly lit lives of everyone else,
        instead of dealing with my own shit.

        My mentions are still a madhouse—
        ten days of internet fame
        with no sign of fading.

            I can't help but wonder why,
            if social media has started to feel shitty
            even when I'm on top,

            why do we bother at all
            with this hot mess of take downs and pile ons,
            the tempestuous and temporary rise and fall?

Multiple accounts are threatening
to dox Eleanor's home address,
her phone and social security numbers.

And, like I did, they're claiming
it's all for the sake of public safety.
#CallOutKearney an attempt
to neutralize a threat.

Suddenly my inbox pings—
an email, the subject line in bold—

    Felicia has sent
    an assignment.

Felicia's Email

Hi, Millie,

Please find below a list of questions in preparation for our interview on Monday. (How much are you looking forward to it! ;)) Please do make it a point to practice—remember that audiences listen to your tone of voice, facial expressions, and body language as much as the content of your answers. My professional advice is to practice them in the mirror, or—better yet—in front of a friend who can vet anything that's unclear or confusing. Best of luck! See you soon!

xxFF

Your report in The Bloom *broke the Lindley Library fire story. High school journalists are often equipped with neither the time nor the resources to do such hard-hitting investigatory work, yet you managed to write a piece with real teeth.*

What role do you see high school journalists having in contemporary media as the face and fabric of journalism keep shifting?

Can you talk about how difficult it was to expose a community member's mistake for the general wellbeing and knowledge of the citizens of Magnolia and why it's important to always tell the truth, even in the face of scrutiny?

While Eleanor Kearney has not been fired from her library position, she is currently on paid leave and is residing outside of town, under the protection of Deputy Sheriff Greenfield, who happens to be your cousin. Do you believe this is a good use of state resources?

Many Magnolia citizens are reasonably outraged by Kearney's inattention and irresponsible behavior, which placed dozens of residents directly in harm's way, and are threatening to file a civil suit against her.

> *Do you find this to be*
> *an appropriate punishment?*

***

Even though I have time to prepare these answers,
this feels like the most unexpected pop quiz.

    Or like a private note a teacher swipes,
    threatens to read out loud to the class.

I don't have answers for Felicia,
and I don't want to have to find them—

    because now I know
    she's not asking the right questions.

***

I feel Mr. Daldry's frown down my neck,
a tuna fish sandwich scent to his breath.

> *Sorry this class is more polygons than paparazzi,*
> *Miss Willard, but you do have to pay attention.*

> *In fact, I should confiscate that phone*
> *and send you straight to the—*

From overhead, the P.A. system squawks:

> *Millie Willard to the principal's office.*

> *Millie Willard to the principal's office.*

The class giggles like glass—
    tiny shards of shiny, sharp sounds.

Daldry and I stare at each other
for one cold, sweaty second—

> how could Principal Keys possibly sense—
> from halfway across the school, no less—
> that I'm in trouble?

Keys's Office

Now, before you dish a sentence out—

I say to Principal Keys
from the unfortunately familiar leather seat
    opposite his desk—

        —I wasn't even disturbing Mr. Daldry's class.
        I was just—

Confusion creeps
into the corners
of Keys's eyes.

Disturbing class? he says.

    No, Millie, I brought you in here
    because we need to talk about something else.

        What exactly is happening with The Bloom?

***

He continues:

First Maya and Lola Sun
ask for special permission to switch homeroom
    for study periods,

    which I granted,
    under the assumption
    they needed a break
    after the hurricane.

        But then Maria Renée storms into my office
        and tells me she's done?

            That she's through with The Bloom
            and wants to hand the editorship over to you?

                That I can fail her for all she cares?

            And then I hear rumors from the printers
            that they haven't seen so much as a proof?

                Is this true, Millie?

                    It sounds like you
                    let Florence tear y'all apart.

***

As Keys talks,
the warm air of my emotions

    rises to the surface of my chest,
    a condensed low-pressure area constricting my lungs.

      It's hard to breathe.

With heavy heaves,
I try not to cry,
but it's too late—

a flood gate of panic and fear
forces hot tears from my eyes.

I can't do it anymore, I yell.

    I can't.

      I can't.

        I can't.

***

Keys scrawls something on a piece of paper,
    his handwriting slender and illegible.

    Probably my suspension spelled out in dark blue ink.

Normally, I read these notes instead of write them, Millie,
but it seems like you need this. Give this to your mom.

    I'm giving you an emotional health day tomorrow.
    I'll let your teachers know too.

Don't worry about coming to class.
Just take care of yourself.

Friday, October 12th

Mental Health Day

I try to prep for my interview,
but it does not go well.

Practice Answers 1

As a journalist, I sincerely believe the people of Magnolia deserve the truth. It's deeper than a belief; it's a conviction that citizens live their safest, smartest lives when equipped with the best information. When I broke the story on Eleanor Kearney's mistake—and it was a mistake, albeit a potentially deadly one with dozens of lives at stake—I had hoped—

> *I had hoped—*
>> *What exactly* had *I hoped?*

Practice Answers 2

*When I broke the Lindley Library story, I had hoped the city would
be smarter and safer in the wake of this new information. I wish
someone would have written a similar story, a call to action for the
South Carolina Department of Transportation to update and install
better road signs before my daddy died. But if we look at the town's
response—who is safer when we issue death threats, channel our
despair and helplessness onto an easy target? Who's smarter? What if
we started asking the right questions, like—*

like—

Practice Answers 3

C'mon, Millie, what are *the right questions?*

I Need Help

I want feedback to figure out what
to say in front of Felicia's camera.

When writing a report, I can edit my words—
draft and redirect any sentences
that aren't sure-footed enough
to stay the course of my meaning.

But during an in-person interview—
I can no more guide the route of my words
than I can a hurricane's rain.

Even with practice,
it's still just a projected path—

what if I slip and say something stupid?

Even though she doesn't trust Channel Five
any farther than the station's small-town signal,

Mama's a straight shooter.

She'll know what to say.

Only problem is,
she's still mad at me.

Apologizing to a Virgo

Mama's shoulders cleave together
    tighter than garlic cloves
    whenever she stands near me—

but maybe reconciliation is worth a shot.

I search how to apologize to a Virgo,
    and, shit, they seem like a stubborn sign.

I text:

    Hey, Mama—I'm sorry
    things have been tense between us.

        I know you're working hard right now
        to make everything perfect for your fundraiser.

            You're good at that,
            organizing and executing events—

                setting standards high—
                only blue-ribbon,
                prize-wining produce on your plates!—

        but, maybe, if you're not home too late,
        you could help me prep for this interview?

Mama's Response

Can't tonight—working overtime at The Anchor.

And then:

Frozen cauliflower pizza in the fridge for supper.

This permission to enter her kitchen
is the closest to kindness I'll get.

Apologizing to an Aquarian

Aquarius might be an even worse sign to have slighted.
Site after site, internet astrologers offer similar advice.

One popular blogger spells it out
to her thousands of followers:

Aquarians are free-spirited,
but not forgiving when spited.

The worst thing an offender can do
to a Water Bearer
is to double-down
on demands for forgiveness.

They need time and space,
their own pace to decide
the path of reconciliation.

Aquarians are loyal
and don't let go of friendships easily—

so all is not automatically lost
if they have grievances with you.

They may forgive,
but they won't easily forget.

I Try Anyway

I text:

Hey, Lola Sun,

> *I want to give you your space.*

> *I know I've upset you,*

> *and you deserve your time to think.*

> *But I also need you now.*

> *If it's okay,*

> *would you be able to help me*

with questions for my interview?

> *There's no one I trust*

> *more than you.*

Her Response

Still nothing.

I Cry Myself to Sleep

A saltwater stain starts small
on the left side of my pillow—

    a dark center, gray edges fade

    like a precipitation circle
    on a meteorologist's surface map.

I cry clouds over larger and larger spaces
of my cotton pillowcase,
    some imaginary town now drowned,
    soaked in my unknowing—

        unknowing how to make things better
        between me and Mama,
            me and my best friend;

        unknowing how to proceed
        with an interview that I'd hoped
        would launch my career;

            unknowing how to honor my daddy's memory
            and make him proud;

                unknowing how to run the newspaper
                I thought I deserved to have.

My sleep is full of fit and fright,
even with Lola Sun's turquoise
slipped beneath my pillow.

    I dream of the storm surge
    that crashed against my car door
    during Florence—

        wake with a shoulder ache,
        a phantom pain so sure of itself

            that my arm feels swollen and sore.

My Last Resort

With no one else to turn to,
I call Ellis.

> An explanation rains out of me,
> rushed words hurried as hail.

>> I explain everything
>> about my stormy semester,
>> the sensation of my story,
>> poor Eleanor, and how I caused
>> her eviction from an outraged Magnolia.

He listens patiently.

> I wait for him to admonish me
> with wise parental advice—

>> to hear the tone of disappointment
>> drone through his end on the phone.

Instead,
    he
    surprises
        me.

***

Ellis asks,

> *What's the first thing you did*
> *to clean up after the hurricane?*

I say,

> *We cleaned debris from the yard.*
> *Drained sewage that seeped up.*

He says,

> *You're talking about the outside, Millie.*
>
> *What did you do to clean up inside?*
>
> *The places where you eat and sleep?*
>
> *What did you do*
> *to clean up the space*
> *that keeps you safe?*

***

He continues:

> *You took stock of what was inside.*
> *Photographed damages for insurance claims.*
>
> > *You wore gloves and masks*
> > *to protect from mold.*
> >
> > > *Opened windows to prevent mildew.*

I say:

> *I don't understand.*

He says:

> *You have to clean up messes from the inside out.*
>
> > *Instead of worrying about what Heather Grace*
> > *or Lola Sun is angry about,*
> >
> > > *you have to fix yourself first.*
> > >
> > > > *What can you do now*
> > > > *that will make* you
> > > > *feel better about this mess?*
> > > >
> > > > > *You're a journalist because you want to help,*
> > > > > *so you have to figure out*
> > > > > *what's your next best step.*
> > > > >
> > > > > *What way can you help others*
> > > > > *that will make you feel proud of yourself?*

***

Ellis adds a final thought:

It's like Heather Grace says, Millie.

One day it'll be four months past Florence.

Don't focus on what feels important today.
It seems a more fruitful question to ask—

> *what will matter the most,*
> *what will make the biggest impact*
> *the more time passes?*

Our Storm Inches Closer to the Shore of Right Questions

When I hang up with Ellis,
I immediately text Stephen and Todd:

Come over to my house tomorrow—it's urgent.

No, it's an emergency.

We're going on the attack.
We're going to figure out
the right questions to ask.

V. One Month Past Florence

Sunday, October 14th

First Thing in the Morning,

Todd and Stephen barrel into the kitchen.

Light spills in from the stained glass behind them—
golden as saffron, scarlet as sumac.

Todd grumbles guttural sounds,
like crunched leaves
falling from their mouth.

Millie, I wanna help and all,
but if I miss kickoff—

They stop talking, Stephen behind them—
mouths open over the plethora
of plated appetizers and entrees
Mama's mapped out on the counter.

Hope you're hungry! she says,
her smile wide.
The highpoints of her cheeks
streaked with flour
and her special
vegan baking grease.

She might still be sore with me,
but she'd never turn away mouths to feed.

***

Mama's been baking every waking moment,
prepping for the fundraiser.

I've never seen her this nervous—
    not even for Florence.

Stephen and Todd go straight for a steaming plate
of biscuits shaped like bats.

Eat up, friends! Mama exclaims,
flourishing a bowl of black bean hummus—
vegan sour cream piped into a spider's white web.

Todd smiles at Mama,
asks, *How'd you get the biscuits
to taste like buttermilk, Mrs. Willard?*

*Why, almond milk
and vinegar!* she beams.

Emily Paige Wilson

I Share the Plan

After they eat a cave's worth
of baked bat biscuits,
        Stephen and Todd settle in
        to listen.

Here's the plan, I say.

My exposé answered the question:

    What—or who—
    caused the library fire?

Now everyone's fixated on the problem,
expects the next feature to address:

    What's a fitting punishment
    for Eleanor Kearney?

But what if we map out an action plan
and ask:

    Why is Magnolia always so vulnerable
    to the threat of natural disasters,

    and—come next hurricane season—
    how do we avoid more catastrophes?

A Category Five Brainstorming Session

Instead of wind, it's overwhelm.
Instead of barometric pressure, it's stress.

So many avenues of improvement
to choose from.

Circles of research—
    concentric,
    overlapped—
            mapped out resources
            and past failed action plans.

The government's botched response
to Katrina and Hugo.

    How has so little changed?

    With so many lives at stake,
    how do we keep making the same mistakes?

We Can't Get Petrified into Inaction,

Todd says.

Perfection is a false asymptote
we'll never reach. We can't solve
all these problems, but that can't stop us
from getting involved.

Let's focus on the good we can do,
what's within our scope and control.

***

The hours scatter through my room—

    like the ideas we pass back and forth,
    reject and revise, refine further still—

until they've somehow spooled themselves
into an afternoon spent—

    a drafted action plan
    for a community-based
    public safety campaign.

This is great and all, Millie,
Stephen says,
        but this is a huge project—
        especially for the three of us
        on a Sunday—

        and you have an interview
        to prep for.

        We'd need backup to succeed—

        we'd need—

            A knock sounds
            at the front door.

***

Two familiar voices float
down the hall—

These don't taste vegan at all!

—and—

But how did you bake
meringue ghosts with no eggs?

With her flour-streaked
and frizzled auburn hair,

Mama looks like Dr. Frankenstein,
as she clangs and bangs around copper pots.

She's caught Maya and Maria Renée
in her crosshairs—
hollerin' at high volume
about something called *aquafaba.*

It's the thick liquid in canned chickpeas—
unsalted, unsalted, of course, Mama chirps.

And while I'm mortified
she's telling them all this,

I can't get over it.

Here. In my kitchen.

Maya and Maria Renée.

Maria Renée Lays an Editorial Eye over the Plans

This is great, you guys!

She beams, and I can see it in her eyes—
    the pride, the surprise—

        that *The Bloom* will continue
        to report great news once she leaves,
        will pollinate the minds
        of Magnolia High students with its pages.

This is a great combination
of individual action
and systemic change—

    those things can be hard to balance, you know?

    How do you encourage people to feel empowered
    while also calling on the larger context for structural shift?

        It's a huge question in activism—

Stephen Cuts In

But do we want journalism
to be activism, Maria Renée?

    I know true objectivity
    doesn't exist,

        but should we protect our readers
        against a conflict of interest?

Maria Renée Responds

As long as any feature
we run about this in The Bloom
sticks to reporting on facts
and leaves room for reader interpretations,
we shouldn't have a problem.

We can volunteer our personal time,
but that will have to be noted
each time we report on the campaign's progress.

How's that?

But a multi-faceted safety campaign
like we're presenting
means we probably need to bring in campus partners.

> *We'll need buy-in from the Climate Change Club,*
> *maybe JROTC, probably the Young Democrats*

> *and even*—she feigns a gulp—
> *the Young Republicans.*

The Five of Us Are Here and Yet—

not everyone.

The one reporter I never thought
would leave my side—

my guide to the galaxy,
my star-chart-reading,
heart-shaped-glasses-wearing,
faux-freckle-drawing—

and then—
another knock on the door.

***

Mama's full-on Frankenstein's monster now
as she mashes avocados to assemble a witch.

To Lola Sun, she says—

> *This big bowl of guacamole*
> *will be her face.*
> > *Black olive eyes,*
> > > *and blue corn chips*
> > > *fastened as her pointy hat!*

Lola Sun laughs.

We may have been fighting,
but not long enough for her to forget
what Heather Grace is like.

Emily Paige Wilson

***

How'd you know we were here? I ask.

A black star is stamped
at the corner of each eye—

    a stencil she filled in
    with a felt eyeliner pen—

        so it looks like she is literally
        rolling her eyes to the high heavens.

Todd texted me.
    Duh.

No offense, Millie,
but you thinking you could stage
an entire public relations operation

    without me—

        that's the most Capricorn thing
        you've ever done.

***

Back in my room,
our team finally complete once more,
Lola Sun speaks about what the universe has in store.

*If we do want to launch
a public safety campaign,
we need to consider what the stars say.*

> *We'll have Venus Retrograde
> in Scorpio until November 5th.*

> *This means a changing of the tides—
> it's high transformation season.*

*Tomorrow—Monday, the day of Millie's interview—
Mercury will be conjunct Venus.*

> *This is a call to action,
> to clear miscommunication.*

*Then all next week, the stars are on our side.
Mercury is square Mars,
      and the Sun enters Scorpio.*

*We can dislodge seeds of strength
from any previous discomfort,
learn how to further fortify
what's fragile in our community.*

*And—get this—Venus
begins a new cycle on the 26th.*

> *The Friday before Heather Grace's fundraiser.*

> *The stars are perfectly aligned
> for a precise turning point.*

Delegating Tasks

We have one afternoon—maybe two
    if Mama lets me skip school tomorrow—
        to set this plan in motion.

As everyone departs to enact
their respective jobs—

    Lola Sun to speak with Mama
    about whether The Anchor
    would agree to our plan,

    Maria Renée and Maya to speak with JROTC
    and then with Sheriff Beatty,

    Stephen and Todd to call on
    all the student clubs we'll need—

I consult my vision board.

This might not be a Peabody-worthy piece,
but I'll be damned if I don't do it right.

Leaving Mama and her mess
in the kitchen,
        I head out to complete
        the plan's hardest part.

I Call Garrett

I know you don't want to hear this,
but I have a way to fix this mess.

I lay out our plan,
point by point,

      ushered out as fast
      as I can in the hopes
      he won't hang up.

         I need you to trust me, I say,
         then wait with bated breath.

What Garrett Says

Let me call the station.
I'll have someone give you a ride.

The Morning of the Interview

Even with everything that's going on,
Mama won't let me miss any more school—
especially a Monday—

    regardless of how I haven't even slept,
    been up all night in Charleston.

    Four months from now,
    it'll be finals, she says,
    sizzling eggless French toast.

        More like two months, I moan,
        melt a square of dark chocolate
        in my coffee,
            a semi-sweet,
          steaming mocha.

Mama squeezes my shoulders with warm hands.

    Don't be worried about today, okay?
    Everything will be fine.

        Do you need me to drop you off?

No, I say, *but thank you.*
Lola Sun's on her way.

    Mama smiles, says,
    Then I'll see you after school.

Social Media Is a Funny Thing

No one was talking
about the interview
this morning.

But then—by lunch—
    a whispering starts.

      Quiet at first,
      like wind whistling through trees—

         then louder,
         like the crunch of leaves
         under jumping feet.

Virtual shouting against Eleanor
that sprout from anger
and spiral into the ugliest shades
of sexism and ageism in their rage.

      I'm glad those high schoolers outed her.
      Next time she returns to Magnolia
      better be to pick a plot for her grave.

      What a waste of government resources
      to keep that bitch safe.

All tagged with *#CallOutKearney.*

I scroll through all the posts
to see who started the buzz—

    and, no surprise—

      none other than Channel Five.

***

As the school day finally finishes,
I leave my textbooks in my locker—
    a folded sheet of paper slips out.

    This you? I ask Lola Sun,
    expecting another star-spun fortune,
    a planet-fueled twist of fate.

    Nope. She shrugs her backpack
    over the slope of her shoulders.
    Not me this time.

The paper is weighted—
    a heavy letterhead.
    Typed even.

    Dear Miss Willard,

    We're all rooting for you.
    We know you'll make us proud.

    P.S. I didn't want to have to call you
    down to my office again
    just to wish you good luck.

    —Principal Keys

The Newsroom at Channel Five

is a frenzied hive of bright lights and bodies.

Around us are green screens
and white cyc walls,

    production control crew
    dressed all in black.

Teleprompters with a screen
of scrolling white text,

    cameras fastened
    to free-rolling pedestals.

The smell of stale coffee and sweat.

A floor manager calls out,

    Talent. Talent.
    Do we have eyes on the talent yet?

      And I realize
        she means
          me.

In the Makeup Room,

Todd and Lola Sun meet me and Mama.

Even though I protest,
    my nose is powdered—

    my brows brushed
    and darkened with pomade.

        For contrast, the makeup artists says.

            Any imperfections you're worried about?
            What about the size of these pores?
            Those bags, all puffy and blue?

        But I wave him off—
            him and Todd and Lola Sun—

        No, no, no, I say.

        No hair straightener—
            no cakey foundation.

            And, sorry, Lola Sun,
            but no stars stenciled near my eyes.

***

The only thing I do want, I say,
is this.

I pull out a bottle of red polish.

Check Together or Separate?

Mama's signature high shine maroon.

Wait! Mama says.
Not that shade.
That's not the one for you.

She hands me a bottle of blue—
a deep, satiny lacquer.

Newsroom Navy.

This, Mama says,
as she hands it to the artist

who buffs my nails
before he paints them.

This is your color.

Five Minutes before Filming

I have my best friends around me,
    my mama,

        good luck turquoise in my pocket,
        and my nails freshly painted.

Talent to set,
please secure talent to set.

      A microphone is clipped
      to my blazer's lapel.

      I'm given a glass of water
      and positioned behind the anchor's desk
      in a guest seat set to the left
         of where Felicia Fitz will be.

           Side chatter falls silent.

            Hot white-yellow lights
            flare up before my face.

My mouth is dry
and my heart races,

but

         now is my chance
         to be the journalist
         I've always wanted to be.

***

To the side of the set,
Mama's breath catches in her chest—

    short and jagged
    like the serrated blades
    she drags through tomatoes.

That can only mean one thing.

Felicia Fitz Glides toward Me

She's real, and she's here—
        all of her.

    The blonde hair teased meaner
    than a temper tantrum.

    Gold bands stacked
        up to her knuckles—
            rings that wink
            when she straightens her papers,
            taps her notes on the podium.

Her accent and perfume
both thick and viscous as honey.

    Her energy busy as a beehive—
    its high vibes,
        its crackling attitude
            of stand back
            or be stung.

***

Millie, she says.

    She draws my name out like a millipede.
    The sound of it crawls wrong on my skin.

I'm so glad you're finally here!

    So—just like you prepared in your notes.
    We'll go through one question at a time.

She squeezes me close to her,
but her shoulder and neck move—tense—
    like she's motioning,
      signaling to someone else.

She's sprayed the floral notes
of some expensive fragrance
near the base of her throat.

    In my ear she whispers,
    You're gonna do just fine.

We Go Live on Air

The lights behind us dim,
then brighten,
      blinding—

         an orange-gold eclipse in my vision.

Channel Five's theme song blares bombastic—
short, spastic trumpet notes.

On a screen across from me,
I see us.
      Felicia behind her desk,
    me on her left—

         a blue news banner
         streaming beneath.

Hello, she says—

    that warm bell of a welcome
    I've watched night after night—

    and welcome to Channel Five News.

    This time a month ago, Hurricane Florence
    ravaged our coast, bringing with it disaster
    and an emergency shelter sent up in flames.

      Here to discuss that with me
      is Millie Willard.

***

People like predictability—
     the comfort of knowing what comes next.

It's why movies are best enjoyed
with a spoiled ending.

     Less suspense, but no unwanted surprise.

It's why people are so quick
to turn to anger and blame
when it rains on a day
a weatherwoman said would be sunny.

I breathe a sigh of relief
as Felicia asks me her first question—

     the one she sent me earlier—

     the one I've practiced for.

My First On-Air Question

Felicia says,

> *Part of what makes the story you broke*
> *so incredible is you yourself, Millie.*
>
> *Sixteen and reporting like a professional.*
> *Truly impressive.*
>
> *What role do you see high school students like yourself*
> *playing in today's journalism?*

I recite what I've rehearsed.

> *Well, Ms. Fitz.*
> > My voice shakes at first—
> > tremors, though—not a quake.
> >
> > I take a sip of water
> > to release the hot unease in my throat.
>
> *The news doesn't not happen to us*
> *just because we're teenagers.*
>
> *Climate change is affecting our generation—*
> *carbon in our air, lead in our water.*
>
> *School shootings occur more and more often,*
> *and all we're offered are the prayers of politicians.*
>
> *If the news is going to happen to us,*
> *then we deserve to report on it too.*

***

Even though I know
what Felicia's second question will be—
    can predict with 100 percent accuracy
    what she'll ask next of me—

    a storm of misinformation
    surges in my mind,

    a chaotic collage
    of malformed memories.

        The panicked preparation before Florence hit.

        Cars littered on the highway, left for fear of floods.

          The river rush that rocked us violent
          in our own minivan, threatened to topple us over.

            The not knowing if we had a home to return to.

            The not knowing.

              The not knowing.

I know which question comes next.

Felicia says,

> *Eleanor Kearney, the emergency shelter staff member*
> *who inadvertently started the flames,*
> *has been the source of much community ire,*
>
>> *especially after old Facebook posts went viral*
>> *in which she essentially blames*
>> *the good people of Magnolia*
>> *for ignoring climate change.*
>>
>>> *Millie, how difficult was it*
>>> *to expose a community member like that,*
>>>
>>>> *when breaking a story*
>>>> *left a broken town so upset*
>>>> *that it led to death threats?*

I Freeze.

Completely.

A Surprise Arrives Anyway

Mischief glints in Felicia's lipsticked grin—
a glitter of *gotcha* in her eyes.

> *I know this must be hard, Millie,* she says.

> She casts a sympathetic glance
> toward the camera.

>> *Maybe it's a good time*
>> *to bring out*
>> *tonight's second special guest.*

Now it's my turn
to be surprised.

> No one ever said anything
> about a special guest.

Mama's Breath Hisses Off-Camera

Not an angry, shaky rattler's hiss—

> just the whisper of a garden snake,
> slithering past greenly in low grass.

What the actual hell? she says.
A "special guest"?
This isn't how real news works.

She's shushed, but still
she spits slurred, rushed words.

> *Damn this woman and her special guest.*
> *Acting like my daughter's*
> *on a cheap daytime soap opera.*

Producers Provide a Third Chair on Set,

while two crew members assist
a middle-aged woman
with wisps of pale pinkish hair.

    A black blazer—

    shoulder pads to high heavens,
    safety pins in a shiny river down the sleeves—

    draped over a faded Cyndi Lauper tee.

Too much blush—

    an electric peach
    polished into the cheeks—

        as if this were 1983
        and the application
        was done in a rush.

Bands and bands of silver rings,
heavy stones, sild onto fingers
stained yellow from nicotine.

    Before me sits
    Eleanor Kearney.

***

Felicia's energy is so charged,
I'm afraid she'll send a sharp static shock
down my arm as she reaches for my shoulder.

Now, Ms. Kearney, she says,
you must have some sense of animosity
for Miss Willard.

Here she pans to the camera—
widens her faux empathetic eyes.

I see now how slick she is.

    This tricky technique
    of seeming to care
    while she tests the limits of her guests.

This is not the kind of reporter I want to be.

She goes on.

    Just as much animosity, if possible,
    as Magnolia has toward you
    for endangering those at the shelter,

        for those sweltering social media posts,
        boasting how we all deserve to die.

        With all of town tuning in,
        Ms. Kearney, what do you
        have to say for yourself?

Eleanor Speaks

I harbor no animosity to little Millie here.
In fact, all I hold in my heart for her
                    is gratitude.

***

This is precisely why people don't like
to be surprised.
       Felicia's eyes freeze over
       with an icy sheen
       we never see on South Carolina roads.

I'm sorry, she says.

       Her icicle eyes
       shoot straight to some poor producer
       who stands in the corner.

              Here's the reporter whose story
              turned your life upside-down,

              and, instead of hate,
              you feel grateful?

It's My Turn to Do the Surprising

I clear my throat,
able to speak in sure-footed syllables
for the first time since the start of the show.

I sit up, push my shoulders back
to straighten my blazer—
    navy polish on my nails,
    turquoise stone in my pocket.

Millie Willard, reporter.

    Allow me to explain, I say.

Our Plan Revealed

I actually met with Eleanor yesterday
for an extended interview.
I believe we have the tape available?

I nod to Todd,
who thumbs-up—
    meaning they were able
    to slide the tape
    into the control room.

If Felicia narrowed her eyes any further,
her faux lashes would fuse together.

    There is no tape—

        She pauses, presses a finger
        to her earpiece, listens
        to someone speak.

        Wow, alright.

          She taps her notes together briskly,
          quickly tries to regain the composure
          I've stolen from her.

          She says, *Let's roll the footage.*

Eleanor's Backstory

Seated in a beige hotel armchair,
the soft, yellow halo of lamplight
a frame around her face,

Eleanor speaks.

My mother took me
to the first Earth Day festivities—
and every year after,
environmental protests, petitions, campaigns.

Is it a memory or a story memorialized?
I'm unsure—but four-year-old me
sat on my mother's shoulders
parading down the streets.

How empowering it was—
this pact to protect our world—
the passing of the Clean Air and Water Acts.

Like we could take the health of the planet back.

I grew up with the belief
that this power was within our reach—

to stop the rise of pesticides,
prevent improper disposal
of dangerous industrial waste.

As a child, my imagination ran wild
with possibilities—mine was the generation
to save the peregrine falcons,
the alligators, polar bears,
the packs of red wolves—

    their russet-furred muzzles,
    their foxlike faces.

She coughs a nicotine-nicked laugh,
throat coated with smoke.

    Hell, I even got arrested once
    for protesting naked for PETA.

    But I believed it.

    We were going to preserve the world.

    We had information.

      We had public buy-in.

        We had enough time.

***

Then capitalism and its pollutants exploded,
and with it, most of my hope.

Nihilism replaced my childhood naivety,
and it all became clear to me—
　　the grim and grimy reality.

Half of all plastics produced
are single-use—

　　　then off to the rivers they're thrown.

　　　We now run the risk
　　　of more plastic than fish
　　　filling our oceans in the next thirty years.

Every second, the earth bleeds
a soccer-field's worth of trees.

　　And I saw a shift,
　　a politicized rift
　　in public opinion.

　　　We're sitting as if our hands are tied
　　　while we watch the rise of carbon dioxide,
　　　our reliance on fossil fuels and cheap meat—

　　　　enjoying the comfort of our front-row seats
　　　　to the natural world's inevitable defeat.

Emily Paige Wilson

***

Deflated at what felt like
the insurmountable fate of the planet,

I started smoking,
started to once again
eat red meat.

> *Occasionally I would vent my anger*
> *in some near-sighted social media posts.*

>> *But, no, I don't think*
>> *anyone deserves to die.*

Even though there is anger and fear.

How the hell does a part-time employee of the state
who doesn't even qualify for health benefits

> *get roped into risking her own neck,*
> *stationed at an unsafe shelter with no training,*
> *no say in being forced to stay?*

>> *But to the town of Magnolia,*
>> *for my inattention, for the split-second decision*
>> *to plug in a kettle and step outside—*

>>> *the guilt, the shame*
>>> *that engulfed my body*
>>> *when I saw the smoke and the flames—*

>>>> *to the town of Magnolia*
>>>> *and all those with me in Lindley,*

>>>>> *I sincerely apologize.*

The Camera Pans Back to Eleanor

Beneath the bright lights of the studio,
her skin seems less smooth—

> the grooves engrained in her face,
> etched in thin lines around her eyes,
> a small-scale spaghetti map on skin
> of where all the storms in her life have been.

The gravel in her voice grates
across the mic clipped to her blazer.

Fear spreads faster than forgiveness.
Despair spreads faster than hope.

And for the last twenty years,
I've been charting my course
on the wrong boat.

> *Talking to these young kids*
> *has given me back a pinhole of optimism*
> *through which to envision a better future.*

> *There are many challenges ahead—*

> *growing pains that will demand of us*
> *to commit to the uncomfortable—*

> *but, with these young people in charge,*
> *I'm proud to endorse and offer continued support*
> *to the Casey Willard Safety Campaign.*

The Casey Willard Safety Campaign

That's right, I say,
staring straight into the camera,
into the living room of everyone in Magnolia,

    my small coastal town
    the hurricanes can knock around
    but can't take down.

The Casey Willard Safety Campaign

    calls upon community members
    to contribute to a collective project
    to make pre-disaster and evacuation
    efforts more effective.

    The campaign is set to go live on The Bloom*'s website*
    tomorrow morning at nine a.m.

***

My speech ends—
and, quite possibly,
my journalism career with it.

I wait for Felicia to throw a fit,
to quit in a cyclone of rage,
to rampage off the stage
after I've sabotaged her report—

    but then—

        applause.

A soft patter at first—
    one or two crew members—
        then a cascade of clapping hands.

        Mama, Lola Sun, Todd.

        The cameraman, the makeup artist.

        An intern even puts down
        the extra-large cups from her coffee run.

        Applause
        loud enough
        to drown out a storm.

***

Felicia's face is blank now,
betrays none of her frustration.

She really is a pro.

To the camera, she says,

> *Well, folks, you heard it here first.*
> *More breaking news live on Channel Five.*
>
> *And we'll be back*
> *after this commercial break.*

The Mic Is Unclipped from My Blazer

Eleanor is escorted off stage.

> A producer says to my mom,
> *That was amazing.*
> *Our ratings are through the roof!*

> Mama beams back.
> *That's my Millie.*

Before I leave, Felicia turns to me.
She says,
> *You've got one hell of a career ahead of you, kid.*
> *It's not often I'm bested.*

I respond,
> *No, Felicia, you're still the best.*
> *I've just learned this is not the way*
> *I want to play the game.*

I turn to my trio,
hug them all and sigh.

> *Let's go home.*

Mama Pulls Out Daddy's Old Shoebox

from beneath the passenger's seat
once the two of us are in the minivan.

> *You remember this?* she asks.
> I nod—his shoebox full
> of old newspaper clippings.

> How he mouthed off
> about the weather reports
> in the margins.

> *I went through it again today*, Mama says.
> *I always miss Casey more on big days like this—*

> *and wouldn't you know it,*
> *but he had something to say?*

I squint, confused, as she slides me
a wrinkled and worn strip of paper.

> The weather report for October 15th, 2003.
> Fifteen years ago, today.
>> In Daddy's rough hand reads,
>> *Well, don't it beat all,*
>> *but that weatherwoman*
>> *was actually right for a change.*

Tuesday, October 16th

Breaking News from *The Bloom*

The Casey Willard Safety Campaign
by *The Bloom* staff

Two weeks ago, *The Bloom* reported on how the fire at Lindley Library, a building with well-known structural issues that was designated as an emergency shelter during Hurricane Florence, was a result of the actions of Eleanor Kearney, a part-time librarian ordered by state mandate to serve as shelter staff during the storm. Kearney plugged an electric kettle into one of the library's ungrounded outlets, which short-circuited when Kearney stepped outside. The kettle sent off sparks that burned down the library's west side, leaving 77 residents and their pets exposed and vulnerable until they could be relocated.

This controversy caused community-wide conversations around public safety and pre-disaster preparedness. It also ignited spirited and oftentimes divisive backlash over Kearney's actions, ranging from social media outcries to death threats serious enough to be considered a real risk by the sheriff's office. Kearney has since apologized, leaving the town to focus on a larger question at hand: How were we left with unsafe shelters and untrained community members forced to serve as staff during the hurricane? To help address some of the issues and inequities illuminated by Florence, a group of Magnolia High School students are launching The Casey Willard Safety Campaign, which will focus on natural disaster communications, transportation, shelter preparedness, and political actions to address climate change.

The Anchor, a local hotel known for its Southern vegan cuisine, proved to be a well-insulated structure during Florence but has never been deemed an official emergency shelter. The campaign is calling upon The Anchor to offer citizens unable to evacuate in the face of storms free stays in the form of vouchers. The initial request is at least 30 days and nights' worth. Those interested in encouraging The Anchor's owner may reach out to him directly or can contact City Council and request the hotel be compensated through taxpayer money in a future referendum. Additional funds raised will be used to provide hazard pay for anyone mandated to stay and serve in Magnolia during future hurricane seasons.

The sheriff's office will also be partnering with the school's JROTC club to design a pre-disaster preparedness action plan. In addition to mapping out possible evacuation routes around those buildings already designated as shelters, this also requires City Council to designate a common point person to oversee emergency communications. This will cut down on confusion if electronic signals become compromised during storm surges and will ensure interoperable communications remain plausible between county, state, and federal branches of government.

Petitions for local public-school principals to recycle retired school buses into emergency evacuation vehicles will begin circulating shortly. Once Lindley re-opens, Kearney will lead public grant-writing workshops for citizens interested in helping Magnolia apply for Pre-Disaster Mitigation Program Funds from FEMA to increase the number of up-to-code shelters in town.

Finally, the school's Young Republicans and Young Democrats will partner with the non-partisan Climate Change Club to demand our state politicians take a stronger stance on climate change. The campaign's goal is to press politicians into a 10 percent increase in the amount of funds allocated to disaster relief. According to last year's state budget, approved by the governor, the Emergency Management Department pulls in less than one million dollars per year, when the state accrues damages of nearly $300 million annually. For comparison, law enforcement across the state receives 200 times more funding. The Department of Public Safety alone draws in $500,000 for highway patrol equipment, which, according to the fine print, was spent on rifles. This 10 percent increase in relief will also include grants specifically to provide aid to undocumented community members who are ineligible for FEMA support. Those interested in placing calls to our state senators to discuss budget concerns can do so at Magnolia High in Room 112 every Tuesday and

Thursday from 5:00 to 6:00 pm. Discussions about potential protests to be held at the state capital are pending.

Millie Willard, staff weatherwoman, initially launched this campaign, named for her belated father who passed in a car accident on an unmarked hairpin turn. While individual staff members are not discouraged from participating in this safety agenda, we will note all relevant activities when reporting on future campaign stories. *The Bloom* remains committed to independent journalism.

***

As soon as I wake

    —orange-pink wrinkles of fog
    furrow the early morning's brow—

        I set my phone on silent.

No notifications.

    No red bubbles near my texts
    to tempt me to check.

        No social media.
        No virtual vindication needed.

If The Casey Willard Safety Campaign
has been picked up
by bigger outlets,

    it will have to circulate without me.

***

I hold a to-go cup of coffee in my hand—

    Mama's made a pumpkin spice blend
    with cinnamon and clove—

        and wait in my driveway
        for a lime-green Beetle.

It arrives with a honk.

    I head for the backseat,
    but Lola Sun nods at me.

Todd sits in the back,
grins sheepishly.
Their hair now shorn short,
striped black and green in the back.

    Get up here, Lola Sun hollers.
    We've decided—at least for today—
    you've earned back the front seat.

Everything Is Finally Normal Now

We walk to homeroom,
and everyone's present.

      It's like a reset button
      has sent us back to August.

Maya and Stephen share a computer screen—
      stressed over how to best frame
      a photo collage for a feature spread.

      Sticky notes of stats and scores
      left on Todd's desk from various coaches.

      And, of course, Maria Renée
      preparing for The Morning Minute.

By Wednesday, the Winds

of my attention have changed.

I cave in a little,
curious and craving some attention.

My follower count
has proliferated again—
    this time, I've hit the low thousands.

I read it all—
    the good,
        the bad,
            the ugly
                texts and tags.

Sweet tweets:

    @MillieWillard, I'm in middle school now,
    but I hope you're still around when I get to Magnolia High.
    I want to be a journalist just like you!

    Left three voice messages to senators today
    all thanks to #TheCaseyWillardSafetyCampaign!

Horrendous headlines:

Teen Reporter Strikes Again—
All Sensation, No Substance.

Gen Z Continues Bogus Campaign
Against Climate Change Boogeyman

Major magazines are even in my mentions,
my DMs,
    and I both wonder and worry
    if they'll ask me to be a cover story.

Yes, it's a big dream,
but I am the girl
who made a vision board,

    who turned Hurricane Florence
    into a story of both disaster
        and—hopefully—a safer path forward.

The Best Part, Though,

is how, slowly but surely,
the response to Eleanor's apology
is softening the minds of some people.

A handful still hold fast to their anger,
those who were most closely connected
to the people placed in danger,

    but most open up
    to how she acknowledged her mistake,
    wants to accept responsibility
    and repay the community how she can.

Damn, one tweet reads,
I'd be pissed if I had to stay too.
Before you heard her story, it looked real bad.
But now that I know what I know,
it's way harder to stay mad.

TikTok, too, has made her interview trend.
Impassioned teenagers mouthing the words
to her speech—
    Mine was the generation
    to save the peregrine falcons,
    the alligators, polar bears,
    the packs of red wolves—

        shaking theatrical fists in triumph.

***

Someone even started a fundraiser—

>t-shirts printed with *Mine Was the Generation*
>*Support #TheCaseyWillardSafetyCampaign*
>stitched in white across the chest—

>>all proceeds to be donated
>>to shelter funds.

When I showed Eleanor, she grumbled,
mumbled something about how swag
wasn't gonna save the world,

>the cost of water for each cotton shirt,

but I could tell she was pleased.

The Silence Breaks at School Too

As I walk down the hall, strangers wave.

Kids tell me how brave I am,
how I've put Magnolia on the map.

Teachers I don't even know
congratulate me, pat me on the shoulder.

I smile at their kindness
but continue straight to homeroom.

> How silly it once was to convince myself
> that I wasn't in a powerful enough position
> to offer my community help,

> especially when the weather
> won't report on itself.

The Bloom's Official Weather Report

While the clouds' gray shadows suggest overcast, it's a particularly warm October day. Forecast is 78 degrees Fahrenheit and real feel is 79 degrees—it's not often we get such perfect symmetry and specificity in our predictions. Wind is coming in at—

Millie Willard to the principal's office.

Millie Willard to the principal's office.

In the Principal's Office

I blink repeatedly at Principal Keys,
say nothing.

> If I'm in trouble again,
> I'm going to make him tell me
> without incriminating myself first.

He hands me a black box—
small, covered in felt.

Inside is a lapel pin—
a barometer edged with a golden rim.

> *STORMY   RAIN   CHANGE   FAIR   DRY*

> The words printed around the circumference of its beige face,
> its black painted needle pointing toward *CHANGE.*

Congratulations, Millie, he says.
It's not often a hurricane
returns to a town its swept through
and offers to clean up the mess it's made.

> *Are you calling me a storm, Mr. Keys?* I ask.

Millie, he teases,
let's hope we never make it
all the way to the letter M
when naming hurricanes.

> *We've barely made it through*
> *five storms this season,*
> *let alone thirteen.*

On Thursday—

the third day after
the storm of my Channel Five performance—
things are mostly back to normal.

Mostly.

Lola Sun and I lay stretched across
my bedroom carpet,

her head hung low over astronomy homework—

more density and brightness calculations
than compatibility and ascendant signs—

as I text Maya.

We check our answers against one another's
for a brutal square-root equation.

Maya's doing better now,
more assured she'll pass math class.

I scratch out a patch of problem solving,
tell Lola Sun I need a break.

In the living room, we turn on the news.

Live with Felicia Fitz.

Millie, Mama calls out,
if you don't get that witch of a woman off my screen—

but then the three of us fall silent,
barely able to believe what we see.

The Storm Shifts

Felicia Fitz—
    her eyes glitzed in a silver shadow,
    her voice dramatic and low—

reports on The Casey Willard Safety Campaign.

Felicia says,

    In light of what could have been a tragedy—
    a frenzied fire in the local library during Florence—

        the town of Magnolia seems to be turning
        that mishap into a positive change initiative.

            Eleanor Kearney, the woman responsible
            for the accidental blaze,
            has partnered with Magnolia High students
            to launch a public safety campaign
            in the wake of the hurricane.

                Some people are even celebrating
                Kearney's courage in receiving criticism
                and being open to change,
                calling her a hometown hero.

***

Well, I'll be damned, Mama says.
She's a hometown hero now, huh?

*From the same reporter who tried
to tear her to shreds.*

   She sighs.

This, girls, is a lesson.

*The tides of public opinion
are a popularity contest.*

   *People like you best
   when you can bolster them up—
      then they'll drop you on the spot
      when you're not worth the cost.*

      *Now come, turn that trash off.
      Help me finish this banquet menu—
      I want y'all to try this new dish!*

VI. Six Weeks Past Florence

A Static Crackle Snaps in the Air

It hums with hushed, excited whispers,
like the crunch of hundreds of leaves
crumpling beneath the fall of feet.

Even the sunshine slants silverish,
    like the gritty glitter of sidewalk dust,
        like a skeleton's rib or a ghost's reflection
        as it slips past an antique mirror—
        its surface smeared, its frame rusted.

Today, the whole world is cast
as if Mother Nature herself
were ready to attend
this Halloween fundraiser banquet
Mama's putting on at The Anchor.

***

And I know this is Mama's time

to shine—

    a chance to put

    vegan cuisine

    more squarely

    on the Magnolia map—

but it's also my chance

to prove I'm a journalist

who can have a real-world impact,

    and that's a chance

    I can't afford

    to let slip past.

***

After school—

    which spooled by as slowly
    as if some sluggish spider
    tried to weave its web
    with four legs instead of eight—

Lola Sun drops me off
at The Anchor to help Mama decorate.

I'll be right back, she says,
practically slams the car door behind me.

    I need to pick up a few costume supplies.
    Do you think the thrift store
    will have a spare pair of bull horns?

I don't tell her
that her current outfit
could pass as a costume—

    silver glitter chunky heels
    and a green feather boa—

    some of the more high-profile pieces
    from her varied wardrobe.

Lola Sun, I sigh,
do I really have to be
the plus-one for y'all's couple's costumes?

She scowls at me
and looks like her mom.

We're not a couple with a plus-one, Millie.
We're three friends, and—
    as lead designer—
I've decided we're going as three matching friends.

    I'll be back in an hour.

She drives away,
and I know she's right.

I was so stupid to see Todd as competition,
especially when they make Lola Sun happy.

After how they both saved me
from my own misdoings,

the least I can do is sport matching costumes.

357

The Anchor Appears Appropriately Haunted

Cobwebs cover the reception desk.

A fog machine billows forth thick clouds of smoke,
which pulse under the soft purple strobe lights.

Plastic spiders slide over and through
the burnished banister of the lobby stairs,
suspended on silver strings.

Spooky music oozes through a sound system—
rain and the haunting rattle of chains.

A banner hangs high, pinned up by bats.

>   *DON'T BE A GHOUL.*
>   *GIVE BACK*
>   *TO FLORENCE SURVIVORS.*

>   A not-so-subtle ask
>   for the guests in attendance—
>   all set to arrive within the hour.
>   Guests who might soon bestow us
>   with millions of dollars of bequests
>   for the safety campaign.

The hotel's owner hasn't agreed to vouchers just yet,
preferring, for now, to collect direct donations.
Less messy, he said, fewer papers to file.

It might not be what we had in mind,
but it's a start.

And if Florence taught me anything,
it's that even a slow start can quickly take off.

I head to the reception desk,
where a young woman's dressed as a witch,

to ask permission
to slip into the kitchen,

when—from that direction—
a shriek eeks forth.

Mama Hollers to the High Heavens

She's in the kitchen,
among the clatter and clang of copper pots,
the whir of blender blades.

She's in a gaudy getup,
some green cylindrical thing
with sprigs sprouting near her face.

Mama, what are you? I ask.

    Oh, Millie!

    She clasps her costume's edge.

    I'm a leek—isn't it obvious?
    But I've spilled sauce on myself.
    Well, shoot, I hope this doesn't stain!

She sees me blink at her,
downright and dumbfounded.

    What? she asks.
    Michelle Obama made turnips cool—
    I can do the same with leeks!

Mama, that only worked
because Michelle herself is cool.

Mama scowls at me
and throws an apron.

    Quit fussing and get to work.

Mama's Menu Is a Spooktacular Masterpiece

The dining hall tables are already set,
gold-plated platters spread
across tablecloths—

    spider webs woven through,
    spun with silver thread.

Her bell peppers steam,
orange and carved like pumpkins.
Stuffed with quinoa.

Guacamole dip made into a witch's face—
    garnished with black olive eyes.
    Blue corn tortilla chips
    frame her head like a tilted hat.

Bowls of butternut squash soup
on which vegan sour cream ghosts float.

The room smells like cinnamon and nutmeg—
the spiced warmth of cider.

It smells like the million bucks
we're gonna raise
to rebuild Magnolia.

Lola Sun Whirls in, Purple and Sparkling

She's wrapped in a shimmery lilac fabric.

    Purple highlight streaked across her cheeks,
    silver stars painted down her arms.

    She holds a vase askew at her hips,
    the same lilac fabric
        falling forward from its mouth—
        a lavender waterfall.

And Todd's dressed up too—
    scales stenciled down their neck,
    sponge-painted shades of sky and teal.

A fish tail's been fastened to their hip,
silver glitter sprinkled all the way down the fin.

    Todd laughs, *The receptionist thought I was a mermaid*
    and Lola Sun got so pissed off.

    It's not my fault, Lola Sun says,
    that people act like they don't know what a Pisces is.

    Wait, wait, don't tell me—
    I say, dreading my fate.

    Lola Sun winks at me.
    Her purple eyeshadow twinkles.

I found those horns, she says.

I Turn into a Capricorn

It takes thirty minutes.

Todd straightens my hair,
then braids it.

> *It really is so pretty, Millie,* they say—

pins it behind my ears
to make room for the bronze horns
Lola Sun glued to a headband.

A brown, full-body leotard, matching tights.

A garland of green leaves
draped around my sleeves,
and the costume is complete.

*Next year, I want to incorporate more of the Chinese Zodiac,
but this will do for now. It's too bad
we couldn't have gotten Garrett in on this,* Lola Sun sighs.

> *Then we could have been
> earth, air, water,*
>
> *and fire.*

Todd flashes a grin.

Yeah, they say, *but we're still lit.*

We groan. We laugh.

We head into the hallway
as guests arrive,

and I'm just as nervous as I am excited
because each time that door opens—

it could be a potential donor walking inside.

Emily Paige Wilson

***

Garrett and Sheriff Beatty stride in,
tip their hats as people wave.

Both men in olive-brown outfits,
their badges buffed, their chests puffed out proudly.

Why aren't you wearing costumes? I ask.

Why, we are! Garrett gasps,
clutches his heart in mock hurt.

> *I'm Sheriff Beatty*, he says—
> *and he*—pointing to the actual Beatty—
> *is my deputy.*

Close enough now to see their chests,
they have in fact switched badges.

The two men cackle.

> I'm so happy to hear laughter

> that I let them think they're funny.

Surprise Guests

Garrett gets swept away by a senator's aide.

Policy and *promise* are whispered,
right after *safety campaign*,
but I hear nothing more
over the roar of people talking—
    champagne bottles popping—
        the deep, dark tones of organs
        over the speakers.

A couple walks in, holding hands
even though their costumes don't match.

    One man dressed in a white sweatshirt
    with red lines squiggled all over,
    a big red *F* drawn across his chest.

    The second man stands inside a miniature house
    held up with suspenders, a *For Sale* sign in one hand.

    In his other hand, a grumpy orange cat
    curled inside a pumpkin-shaped plastic bucket.

    It's Thayer and Ellis!

I'm Even Happy to See Jasper!

What are y'all doing here? I ask.
　　They wrap me in a hug.

　　I'm a midterm paper—can you tell? Thayer asks.

　　　　Ellis beams at me.

　　We're so proud of you, Millie.
　　We knew you'd do the right thing.
　　Casey would be pleased—
　　　　we know Heather Grace is.

　　Speaking of, where is she?

　　　　They head straight to the kitchen to find Mama
　　　　while Jasper scowls as he's hauled away.

The Bloom Crew Walks In

as the music track
hits a thunderous boom,
a witchy and wild cackle.

They, too, came as themselves.

Maria Renée in a ball gown,
tiara on her head,
satin winner's sash across her shoulders.

Maya in all black,
a camera strapped to her back,
photographer's badge clipped to her chest.

Stephen simply in a t-shirt stamped with *Google*.
I'm a search engine, he says,
or maybe an intern—haven't decided.

Lola Sun whispers to me,
*They'd all look so much better
if they let me put glitter on their faces.*

We head to the dance floor,
ride out this past month's excitement.

A natural disaster and its dreadful aftermath.

A brush with show business and stardom,
a scandal that could have overpowered us.

We dance like it's not a Monday night.

We dance
like there are
storm winds
at our backs.

***

The night slides on—
    hours punctuated purple, then red—
    strobe lights keeping time overhead.

Principal Keys is here, dressed as Obama.

He drinks punch with Mr. Daldry,

    who is a protractor—
    a curved cardboard cutout
    fastened across his shoulders,
    one-hundred-eighty dark lines to mark degrees.

Even Eleanor pops in for a few minutes.
Teased hair, fishnets, and combat boots.
Neon bangles from elbow to wrist.

    It's impossible to guess
    the inspiration behind her costume—

        Madonna? Debbie Harry? Blondie?
        Is this just how she dresses?

        She mostly stays to herself,
        and some people avoid eye contact,
        but more often than not,
        she's met with a wave of half-raised hands,
        shy smiles, and polite nods.

Mama's menu's been a hit,
not that she's been out of the kitchen
long enough to notice.

People pleased, napkins stuffed with snacks in hand.
I can't believe it's vegan! How does this taste just like cheese?

Everywhere I look, people are happy.
Chatting. Dancing.

Signing donation slips
to enter a raffle—

win the chance to learn Heather Grace's secret recipes.

I slip the money Ellis gave me a month ago
to repair my broken phone
into the relief fund.

Florence tried to bring my town to its knees,
but we stand taller than before.

This is the Magnolia we were before the storm,
but somehow even better now.

Well, Isn't This a Disaster

a tall green leek asks from behind me.

My heart stops.
This night is nothing short of perfect!
What could Mama mean?

As I turn around, she smiles.

Don't scare me like that, Mama.
That's mean!

I'm sorry, Millie, she laughs.
She slides a stray strand of hair
behind my horns.

But, she says, *I do have some bad news.*

***

What with this being a big event and all,
Mama says, *we were scheduled to have media coverage.*

Channel Five was set to be here this evening.

Mama smirks with a snarkiness
set somewhere between mean
and straight-up evil.

I wonder why Felicia Fitz
would cancel on us last minute?

>This time, it's a white-gloved hand
>that rests gently on my shoulder.

>The rustle of a sequined dress behind me.

>*That's okay, Mrs. Willard,* Maria Renée says.
>*We'll get this story covered. Front page.*

>She squeezes my shoulder and smiles.

>*And I have the perfect reporter in mind.*

VII. Four Months Past Florence

I Revise My Vision Board

for the start of spring semester.

    All my favorite journalists remain,
    but now I'd never consider
    putting Felicia up here,
        even though she taught me a lot
        about what journalistic integrity is
        and what it's not.

          How the best stories are written
          when you start with the right questions.

    The college seal for Chapel Hill still sits center,
    bright and sky blue.

        After Florence, their journalism program
        sent a scout to our school to interview me.

        Even though I'm a junior,
        they mentioned scholarship options
        if I enroll early admissions next year.

I pin new pictures up:

    Mama in her leek costume,
    me with a wide smile in between Ellis and Thayer
    the night of The Anchor banquet.

        We didn't quite bring in the millions that night,
        but we did raise enough to help Maria Renée's family
        rebuild their roof and send her off to school.
        She's all set to move to NYU in the fall.

We're still negotiating with The Anchor
to turn the rest of the money into shelter vouchers,
especially for those folks who don't qualify for FEMA.

The posters from Eleanor's
grant-writing workshops
in the Lindley's restored west side.

A letter of excellence from last semester
signed by Principal Keys.

A photo from Lola Sun and Todd's
three-month-anniversary dinner,
when Mama baked them a vegan cheesecake.

A headline from *The Post and Courier*—

    how news of our mission to make Magnolia safe
    spread all the way to Charleston's daily paper.

The folded and faded weather report
on which Daddy wrote about how
that weatherwoman was right for once.

And, finally, the new masthead for *The Bloom*,
most of the positions still the same—

    Todd and Lola Sun, Stephen, and Maria Renée's—

    but mine and Maya's have changed.

We're now Co-Assistant Editors,
training to take over in the fall.

Maya passed Daldry's class
and has all the math credits she needs,
so she can breathe freely.

We've also agreed that she'll keep taking photographs
and I'll keep telling students whether to expect sun or rain.

    Between our reports and The Casey Willard Safety
        Campaign—

    some students have already convinced City Council
    to convene for a special safety summit next week—

    we're gonna make Magnolia safer come next hurricane
        season.

Lola Sun beeps her Beetle's horn outside.
Twice to let me know it's really time to go.

    Today is chilly but bright,
    and I have a weather report to write.

Acknowledgments

Thank you, first and foremost, to my agent, Ammi-Joan Paquette, who never gave up on this book, even after two dozen rejections had stolen all steam from me in the cursed years of 2020 and 2021. Even before being a champion during the submission process though, thank you for giving me a project I could hope for and believe in during those transitory years post-graduate school. Sneaking away on lunch breaks during shifts to write a hundred words at a time and using the commute to the community college where I adjuncted to brainstorm a scene or line kept me rooted in the belief that I could take on projects I'd never considered, and that I could develop the craft, through practice and multiple bad drafts, to deserve your time and thoughts as my agent. I don't know which goddess lent a helping hand to bring one of my tweeted poems to your attention back in 2017, but I am very grateful.

To Danys, my editor. Thank you for being a champion for this work and its characters, especially during the acquisition process. There's something magical about learning someone was rooting for your work behind the scenes, and it means a lot to me. Thank you for your time and thoughtful insight with this book. Thank you to everyone at Andrews McMeel.

To Eli, my husband and "anxiety editor" who offered encouragement and grounding through all the disappointment and doubt this process offered. I'm glad we also get to share in the excitement and triumphs together too. Thanks for moving across the country twice with me, even if you did temporarily lose me during the Break Down in Big Timber. To the Sahm family and OBX crew I married into, thank y'all so much for being the funniest, rowdiest group of people I could have lucked into as in-laws.

To Maggie, my double Scorpio best friend. Thank you for never giving up on me or any of my dreams. Remember when we sat in a Barnes & Noble in February 2019, and I ran over the pitch for this book before sending it to Joan? Your Duncan Hines is never irrelevant to me.

To Kathryn, Geniann, and Jessica, thank y'all for being the best set of friends since 2004. Thank you for pressuring me into actually having a bachelorette party. Thank you for making me an aunt to seven beautiful little ones. If this book is past its prime by the time they start reading YA, I promise to write more. Strangely, slowly, shortly, & sparkly.

Of course, to Roy and Joseph, who sheltered us during the storm. Had we not had you, Eli and I would have had to drain all our savings to pay for hotels during evacuation. Thank you for the Netflix and Kemp parties, the coffee from Gwendy's, and for always being our friends. We would have been far less equipped to deal with all the uncertainty and fear without your friendship.

To Laura and Michelle for being the brightest part of Wilmington after graduation. Thank you for the delicious meals every week. Speaking of homemade pasta, I recently learned how Eli thought pasta "grew." Remind me to tell y'all. Thank you to Michelle for helping those in the shelter during Florence and for serving as the loose inspiration for this story. Thank y'all both for keeping Eleanor up past nap time so we could meet her. I hope it's okay I borrowed her name.

To my patrons Alex M., Bailey J., Jan S., and Maggie A. for supporting me consistently over the past two and a half years. I truly appreciate your positivity, enthusiasm, and accountability in the process of writing this project and others. I hope the behind-the-scenes peeks offer you some form of encouragement and enjoyment, because that's the least I owe y'all.